BIG SKY SIREN

BY

L. A. RAMIREZ

ISBN Print: 978-0-9864001-1-7

ISBN Ebook: 978-0-9864001-0-0

The dedication: To my husband Jorge. Thank you for your love, inspiration and confidence. If not for your encouragement, I would never have been able to bring this to fruition.

CHAPTER 1

KEEVA RYAN DROPPED her forehead on the palms of her hands. She knew her friend meant well, but after a long day of work, her back ached and her feet felt like someone had put hot coals in her shoes. She wanted a hot bath, not a night out.

"Keeva, come on, everyone is meeting at Rick's Bar for a drink. You are being such a stick in the mud." Lucy stood, one hand hanging on to her shouldered purse, the other holding the rear door of the kitchen open.

Keeva raised her head from her hands, trying not to convey her frustration. "I'm not being a stick in the mud. I have a business to look after and things to finish up here."

She thought of the long list in front of her and the

hours it would take to get through it. She searched Lucy's eyes, and all she could read was concern. "You go and have fun. Tell the girls I say hi. I promise I'll go next time," she tried softening her tone.

Lucy's gaze shifted to the floor, disappointment evident in the shaking of her head. She pursed her lips before looking back at Keeva, "That's what you said last time."

Keeva knew her life had become tedious, even boring, but she had a business to run. Trying to find patience she didn't feel, she closed her eyes and began counting to ten.

The old wooden screen door of Queen City Café slammed, and Keeva jumped, her shoulders wincing up while her hands smacked down on the tall, wooden work table. "Damn it." Walking to the now empty doorway, she closed the heavy inner door.

A pain began behind her left eye; the start of a headache she knew would exacerbate the stress of the upcoming work. Lucy, her best friend and manager of Queen City Café, deserved to hear the truth about finances, but Keeva could not think of a good reason they both needed the burden. She sighed, staring at the inventory, mentally adding the supplies she needed and weighing the total against the bank account balance. Her shoulders slumped. A night on the town would worsen her predicament.

Three hours later, in the upstairs office, Keeva shut

off the computer. Having walked to work, she dreaded the walk home. She didn't worry about crime in Capital City, Montana, but her tired fatigued muscles already protested from the effort of standing, never mind walking two miles.

She stretched, then eyed the window seat overflowing with plump cushions, telling herself a few minutes' rest wouldn't hurt. Wrapping one of her grandmother's quilts around her shoulders, she snuggled into the cushioned seat.

As the tranquility of early sleep enveloped her, a loud thud shocked her awake. Bolting upright, she blinked to ward off confusion. She listened but didn't hear anything now. What could it have been? The old building had many creaks and groans, but Keeva was sure the sound she had heard had been louder than the normal settling of aging trusses.

She walked through the upper floor, turning lights on as she checked each room. Nothing looked out of place. Maybe the noise had come from downstairs.

Keeva leaned over the wooden railing and saw nothing unusual so she made a slow descent down the stairs. Stepping off the steps into the dining room, the slap of cold air startled her. Had the furnace gone out again? The hall light cast eerie shadows over the unlit room, but provided enough illumination for she to see everything in the dining room. Nothing looked out of place.

"Lucy, is that you?" she spoke to the kitchen door. Not getting a response, she moved closer. Still unsure of the noise, she called, "Tighe?" She wondered if the night baker had come in on time, instead of his usual late arrival.

Entering the kitchen, she flicked the light switch. A blazing white glare from the industrial light blinded her. As her eyes adjusted, she saw the back door standing wide open and hoped the thump she had heard had been the door blowing open. She remembered shutting it earlier, though most days she never bothered locking it from the inside. There had never been a need to. Perhaps it had been the wind. One night last week she'd found the door open, and she'd attributed it to the blustery weather. Casting a glance out the kitchen's lone window, the tree branches remained unmoving. Moving to close the door, she spotted the tall baker's rack, pushed over and the pans it had held scattered on the floor.

She froze. She was unable to move them as the realization someone had entered the café sunk in. But why would someone break into the cafe?

She recalled the cash she kept in the safe. Keeva gulped, unable to take a breath. If someone took the cash, it could mean the end of her business. Every penny she'd inherited had gone into purchasing and remodeling the café. A tightening in her stomach rose and constricted her throat. Tears pushed at her eyes at the thought of losing everything she cherished.

She ran up the stairs and slid to her knees in front of the safe. It looked locked. Feeling a small thread of relief, her trembling fingers fumbled over the round knob. She heard the click, but hesitated before opening the small door. Seeing the envelope, she grasped it and clutched it tight to her chest.

Her relief was short lived at the recollection of the scene downstairs. Someone had entered the café and brought renewed concern. Maybe it had been some teenagers playing around or someone looking to get out of the cold. Neither scenario made sense. She often worked late and the night baker came in at midnight; the surrounding buildings were all nine-to-five so they would be empty at night. Why would someone sneak into the occupied café rather than one of the unoccupied buildings?

She pulled the utilitarian pocketknife from her pocket, flicked it open and secured the lock. The small blade wouldn't cause much damage, but it gave her a sense of security as she moved through the building rechecking the locks. By the time she stepped back into the kitchen the temperature had dropped. She rushed to the door and closed it with a slam, locking the handle and deadbolt.

Nausea rolled in her stomach. She would have to call the police. She didn't want to make an issue of it, but she had to. If the intruder had stolen something and she didn't report it, the insurance company would question her lack of action.

As she dialed the number, a sharp high-pitched, female scream from the vicinity of the alley across the street pierced her ears. She jumped. "What the hell?"

CHAPTER 2

TWO HOURS LATER, Detective Antonio Salazar left the chaos of the hospital and headed for the crime scene. The visit to the hospital and the interaction with the victims' anguished family burned in him like the bitter coffee he drank. The fiery acid ate at his insides as he vowed to find the monster who had caused so much grief.

Seventeen-year-old Todd Nystrom, face ashen and a turban of gauze wrapped around his head and tubes protruding from every part of him, looked more like a cadaver than a young man who had practiced football six hours earlier. The visit had given Tony little information. The teen was an average student who loved football and his girlfriend. Now he lay in a hospital bed, his body see-sawing between life and death. Mrs. Nystrom had looked as pale as her son and had stood immobile at the foot of the bed. Mr. Nystrom had bent over his son as wracking visceral sobs had shuddered his large torso. The mental image of the two parents had left Tony shaken.

Todd's girlfriend, Madison, who had been with Todd when the attack happened, had been too hysterical to give much information. She hadn't seen who had attacked them in the alley and didn't know why they'd been singled out.

Tony reached the scene of the attack and pulled the car up to the curb. Glaring lights, set up at the crime scene illuminated the entry to the alley. Except for the innocuous glow of lights from the building across the street, little else lit the neighborhood.

Dispatch had told him a café owner had found the kids after hearing the screams and had called it in. The call had come in at one a.m., waking him after three hours of sleep. He rested his head against the seat's headrest and closed his eyes. His eyes stung, feeling like they had little bits of glass scratching them. The few hours of sleep was beginning to take its toll. He pried his eyes open. "*Coño,* if people would just go home at decent hours, none of this crap would happen," he mumbled to himself as he maneuvered his large frame from the car.

Tony knew it could be worse. After the violence in Afghanistan and dangerous covert operations in Eastern Europe, he chose to go back to a quieter life in

Big Sky Country, Montana. Ten years of his life, first with the Army's Special Forces Force and then with the CIA's Special Activities Division, soured his dream of saving the world. The last few years in the CIA had become solitary. He lived in cheap back alley apartments in unmemorable foreign cities where the supply of scumbags never seemed to run out. Too many of his friends had died believing as he did. It pained him to the point of avoiding close friendships.

Breathing in the cold air, he looked around at the seemingly quiet neighborhood. The senseless trauma he saw tonight was not as bad as some other crimes he had seen, but the depravity of the attack sullied the normally safe city.

The crime scene tech looked over at Tony, motioning him over. A police officer stood military erect at the entrance to the alley. Tony recognized him as the department's newest rookie. "Are you the first responder?" Tony asked.

"No, sir. It was Officer Smith. He asked me to keep any curiosity seekers away. He's looking for evidence on the other side of the alley."

Tony looked around the deserted neighborhood and suppressed a laugh. He had an immense hatred for the bigoted Smith, but he had to give him credit for his creativity in keeping the rookie out of the way. He shook his head in disbelief.

Tony moved over to shake hands with the crime scene technician, "Find anything, Gary?"

Gary shook his head, the bright lights shining on his white hair.

"Whatever hit this kid is not here. My guess is the perp took it with him and dumped it elsewhere."

He pointed to a darkened doorway, "I think he stood in there and hit the kid from behind." Gary swung a flashlight toward a large blot of a dark liquid. Tony guessed it to be the teenage boy's blood.

"From the location of the kid's injury, he definitely was hit from behind. How's the victim anyway?"

"Todd, his name is Todd."

An agonized helplessness blanketed Tony and the tension squeezed his chest. He sucked in the cool air in an effort to wash away the oppressing feeling. "Other than he has a fractured skull and a subdural bleed, right now they aren't saying much." The memory of the devastated parents was still fresh in his mind, making it impossible for him to shake the helpless feeling. "He was still unconscious when I left."

A small object close to the edge of the police tape caught Tony's eye. He stepped closer to get a better look, using his flashlight to illuminate the object. He could see a small plastic purple cap. He signaled to Gary with a wave of the light as he continued speaking. "Doctors say his young age and good health are all in his favor but it's still touch and go." The teen's battered face and the cautious words from the operating surgeon still gripped Tony. "They were flying him to Denver when I left."

Gary picked up the object, eyeing it with scrutiny. "It's a cap to a syringe." He placed the evidence in a bag. "May or may not be related, but let's hope it gives us more than we have so far. Did the girl ever calm down enough to talk? When I got here, they were taking her to the hospital. She was hysterical and irrational. It would sure help us if she can give us information on the perp."

"They medicated her. I'll try again tomorrow." He looked at his watch and saw it was already tomorrow. He rubbed a hand over the muscles coiled in his neck. Maybe he could get a few hours sleep before he started more interviews.

Tony turned to face Officer Jimmy Smith, who walked up behind them. Neither man offered to shake the other's hand. Tony swallowed down a vitriolic comment and maintained his neutral composure. "Were you the first on the scene?"

"Yes, I took the call." Jimmy pulled out a small notepad from his pocket and read the details of the call.

He looked up at Tony, "I got the call, and being nearby, got here before the ambulance. I didn't see anyone but the two victims and the caller, Keeva Ryan."

Tony waited, but knew Smith would give the minimal information. Jimmy consistently tried to make life as difficult as possible for Tony and never made their working together easy. "And what did you find when you arrived on the scene?"

"The female victim kept yelling about some man attacking them. She couldn't or wouldn't give any more information." Smith looked at Tony, his face bland and emotionless.

Tony balled his fists, an involuntary reaction to the increasing irritation at Smith's lack of sympathy for the victims. "Do you think she held back on purpose?" Tony's quiet voice masked the frustration twisting inside him.

"No, she said the guy bumped into the boyfriend and cursed him. Then she said she didn't remember."

Tony seethed at having to drag the information from Smith. He clenched and unclenched his fists. "What about the caller? And give me all the information." The two men stared at each other.

Without looking at his notes, Smith said in a monotone, "That's Keeva Ryan. She owns the café across the street." With the pad, he pointed behind Tony.

Tony turned and looked at the Victorian house behind him. An unlit sign hung from the porch; the dark building looked as dismal as Tony felt.

"She said she heard the scream and called 9-1-1.

She'd hung up before hearing another scream, grabbed a flashlight and ran toward the sound. Running into the alley, she saw a tall male," he looked at his notes, "about five-eight to six-feet tall, wearing a dark hoodie." His hand with the notepad dropped to his side and he continued in the same disinterested monotone. "Ms. Ryan said the attacker had the girl grabbed by the arms, pulling her backwards, but then he dropped her and ran," he pointed to the end of the alley, "as soon as she shone the flashlight on him. I didn't see anything or anyone when I got here. We'll have to wait for daylight to look a little further. She said she saw the boy on the ground, and after checking for a pulse, she called 9-1-1 again to let them know the location of the victim."

In Tony's experience, people fled or ignored screams. Few brave souls ran into danger. This witness had saved both those kids lives. He was glad there weren't three dead bodies.

"Where is she? You didn't let her leave, did you?" He made his distrust of Smith obvious.

Tony's quick rise to detective remained an ongoing dispute that smoldered between them. Smith had been unequivocal in voicing his anger about an outsider moving up the ranks as fast as Tony had. Several of the other officers confided to Tony that Jimmy's real anger developed from a militia upbringing, leaving him prejudice and fearful of anyone who had a government background. Tony preferred to ignore Jimmy's sarcasm, but Smith's anger often boiled over into their work, forcing Tony to deal with it.

"Listen, Salazar, I," he poked a finger on his own chest, "am from here. I know this town and these people. If Keeva says she's at the café, she'll be at the café. She has enough shit going on with her brother. She doesn't need any more trouble."

Tony felt he'd rather wrestle a bear than continue any discussion with Smith, but the mention of the woman's brother having troubles piqued Tony's interest. "What about her brother?"

"Maybe you should let me get back to my job and go do yours." Smith's voice turned harsher as he glowered at Tony. "Ask her yourself." He turned and sauntered away.

"*Come mierda.*" Tony mumbled the word low, but didn't care if Smith heard him, since Smith was clearly a dumb-ass. A bit louder he replied, "Don't worry, I intend to."

*

Sitting in his car, he closed his eyes and let the beautiful woman's face drift into his mind. He wanted to relive the moment he'd first spotted her.

He was in the alley. He had hurt before, but never people. The control and power he'd felt when he'd terrified and inflicted violence on animals had always thrilled him. Tonight had been different.

He felt omnipotent holding up the pipe and a sensation of ecstasy as the metal cracked the boy's skull. When the boy fell and copious blood had oozed from his head, he felt alive. As if a powerful deity struck him with power, surges of adrenaline shot through every part of his body.

But the stupid girl screamed, draining his elation. He had planned to give her the drug, snatch her and have a grand time later. But her hysterical screaming forced him to shut her up, and he tried to cover her mouth. The little bitch kept fighting him.

While he struggled to stab her with the syringe, the ethereal goddess ran into the alley. He had all the control, the power to decide who lived and who died and then the vision of beauty dashed toward him. She insisted he let the screamer go, but he could hear the control, the strength in her voice. He closed his eyes, wishing he could hold her voice in his head. She sounded so unafraid.

He wanted to talk to her to find out who she was, but he heard the sirens and ran. It didn't matter. He was awkward and would embarrass himself anyway.

Sprawling himself motionless in the tight space beneath the hedges, he ignored the thorny branches that scratched at him. The grassy location behind the alley offered good cover and the higher elevation provided a perfect view to the scene below. From his hiding place, he watched her and got to know her from a distance.

She stayed with the boy. Taking off her sweater and pressing it to his head to curb the flow of blood. When the ambulance took the boy, she turned her attention to the girl, holding and calming the screaming idiot.

He rested his head on his crossed arms and peered through the bushes. For the first time since his mother's death, he felt pleasure. Pleasure gained from the small act of watching the exquisite woman. So brave and perfect, her actions sent an ache to his groin. He had never had the chance to know a woman who fought back. Most women were weak. Even at her own son's expense, his pathetic mother had always obeyed his abusive father.

The cops pried the shrieking girl from the woman's strong arms and moved her to a waiting ambulance. The flashing lights illuminated the scene. He couldn't make out the face of the cop who rushed back to the woman, *his* woman, and it angered him to see any man so near her.

He had never known a woman so confident. Not like the beauty that had materialized before him. She was brave and strong and except for himself, no one deserved to be in her company.

Pain shot through his clenched jaw, but it was a good pain. It kept him focused. After talking to her and taking notes, the cop walked her across the street and shook her hand before allowing her to enter Queen City Café. His stomach tightened and heat crept up his face, as he watched him send her away. He would never have let her leave.

The damp cold ground began seeping through his sweatshirt, and he felt the wet blood that had spattered his chest. He shivered but dared not move yet. He closed his eyes to picture his beauty, and the shaking eased.

When the ambulances and several of the police cars left the scene, he slid from his spot and crept behind the bushes away from the police and their bright intrusive lights. Careful to remain hidden in the cover of the shadows, he pulled his hood back up. A safe distance from the scene and any risk of anyone noticing, he began the half-mile jog back to his car.

A siren, passing several blocks from where he sat in his car, pulled him from his reverie. He sighed. He knew what he wanted. Now he needed a plan.

*

Tony walked the short distance from the alley to the café. As he reached the old building, its pale yellow color and white trimmed porch became visible. The large white porch, trimmed in detailed wooden gables, appeared inviting even with the lack of summer furniture. Lace curtains decorated the windows, fitting the character of a Victorian building. He felt encouraged.

The café owner's concern for detail would prove useful in what she remembered seeing tonight.

The only visible lights glowed from windows located in the back of the building, so he approached the back door. He stepped up the few steps and knocked. The door swung open. A man who appeared to be in his mid-forties, with a paunchy belly hanging over his jeans and homemade tattoos darkening his arms, stood in the doorway. From the white apron the man wore, Tony guessed him to be the baker. Could he also be the café owner's brother?

Tony held up his ID, "Capital City PD, I'm Detective Salazar." He placed the ID back in his pocket, "I'm looking for Keeva Ryan."

"Yeah, she's here. What d'ya want with her?"

Something about the man's unfriendly attitude, along with the homemade tattoos struck Tony. In his experience, people were only hostile to police for a few reasons and none of them good. He made a mental note to find out more about him.

"She witnessed a crime and I need to ask her a few questions."

The man stood immobile for a few seconds before answering. "I'll get her." He let go of the door, letting it swing shut.

Tony's radar, already on alert, yelled a warning. The man had made it clear he didn't like Tony's presence and that could only mean he had something to hide. Tony blocked the door with his foot and pushed it open. "Mind if I come in, it's a bit chilly out here." Without waiting for an answer, he stepped inside. His patience for assholes had run out with Smith.

"Excuuuse me, Dee-tec-tive. How could I forget my manners for Capital City's finest." He turned and walked away.

As soon as he stepped inside, Tony could feel the heat from the large baking ovens. Their warmth felt comforting after the outside chill. The sweet yeasty aroma of baking reached him and his stomach growled.

The baker had left him alone in the large baking kitchen. Tony noted the sleek industrial room, which contrasted with the Victorian exterior. The neatness of the place supported his previous speculation. Ms. Ryan would be a stickler for detail, bolstering his hope he'd gain useful information from her.

Tony pulled a toothpick from his pocket and chewed on it, the action filled the eternal minutes before the baker reappeared. Everything about the man sullied the room. Between the lousy tattoo and his frosty attitude, Tony wanted to deck the guy. "She says to go upstairs." The baker used his thumb pointing behind him toward swinging doors.

He removed the toothpick from his mouth and rubbed the back of his neck. "Don't let a little crime interrupt your night," he chided. He wondered what god he'd pissed off. Why else did he have to deal with two heartless imbeciles in the same night? The baker ignored Tony and turned toward the ovens.

At the top of the stairs, shafts of light streamed from two doors. The door further down the hall had a smaller beam of light peeking from the bottom. The sound of water came from the farthest room.

He stepped up to the room that had a light on and an opened door. He found it empty. He needed a moment's peace in case Ms. Ryan turned out to be as hostile as the baker was. Letting out a sigh, he leaned back against the doorframe and closed his eyes. Hurry up and wait, appeared to be the theme of the night.

The image of Todd's pale face filled his mind, but then it morphed. It wasn't Todd anymore, it was Jerry, his best buddy. Jerry's wide grin and blue eyes stared at him, then the image turned to horror when a bright exploding light burst in front of him and the smell of blood permeated Tony's nostrils.

His eyes popped open and he bolted upright. Panting, he looked frantically around the room. It all looked normal. No explosions. No blood. Nothing but a quiet room.

His head throbbed like a war drum whose warning signal slowed as he tried to prevent the flashback from returning. Though Todd had been much younger than Jerry's twenty-six years, the resemblance of their innocent faces was haunting. Tony didn't know if Todd had seen his impending attack, but Tony had seen Jerry's face the instant he knew he was going to die.

"Hello, Detective." A soft, sleepy voice came from the door.

He turned toward the voice. Tony had expected someone much older. Keeva Ryan looked to be in her late-twenties. She was beautiful. Tall and solid, she had dazzling green eyes highlighted by purplish circles underneath. In spite of the late hour, her eyes glinted bright when her pink lips turned up to offer him a smile.

"I'm Keeva Ryan." She held out her hand. "Tighe, my night baker, said you wanted to talk to me."

Curls of brown hair with blonde tips, popping out of a ponytail, framed her porcelain skin. He fought an urge to push them into place.

"Are you okay?" Keeva asked. Her head tipped, and he thought he read confusion in her eyes.

Way to go, stupid. She's had one hell of a night and here you are acting like you're on your first time out to bat.

"My apologies, it's been a bad night. I'm Detective Salazar." He returned the firm hand shake. "Sorry to wake you." He nodded in the direction of the rumpled blanket in the middle of the bed.

"You didn't wake me, Detective. I tried to get a little sleep, but I can't get the picture of Todd out of my mind."

Brave and caring, she continued to impress him. Knowing there were people who did the right thing began to lift Tony's spirits. "Can you tell me about tonight?"

Her chest rose as she took in a deep breath, letting it out as she began to speak. "When I ran into the alley, I yelled. I'm not positive of all I said but it must have worked because he let go of Madison and shoved her towards me. She ran, grabbing me and crying hysterically. Who wouldn't be?" Keeva bit her lip and began moving the cross on her neck in a rhythmic swing. "I held her and made her look at me until she calmed enough to tell me her name. She began sobbing, repeating the boy's name, then she found the strength to yell, telling me I needed to help him. It was all so quick, I still wasn't sure where Todd was."

Her hand stopped and she balled the cross inside her fist. Silence filled the air between them. "Madison began pulling my arm, begging me to help Todd and that's when I saw him. My God, there was so much blood, it was awful." Keeva aimed her tear-rimmed eyes at Tony. He knew the horror she'd seen tonight, a memory he wished he could erase. Maybe when they caught the perp she could begin to forget.

"Madison became more hysterical when she saw the blood, telling him to wake up, nonsensical stuff. I was trying to stop the bleeding and it seemed like an eternity before I heard the sirens and the police arrived."

Tony understood the late hour and stress had begun their stranglehold, but a fresh memory would provide more details. This wasn't the time to quit. "Can you go over the situation from the first scream you heard, anything you might remember about the guy?"

Keeva blew out a breath. "I need some coffee, do you mind if we go downstairs? I think the pastries should be done by now."

Tony remembered his growling stomach. He extended his arm and indicated Keeva should lead the way.

*

Keeva balanced the plate of pastries in one hand, the other paused on the swinging door leading to the dining room. She hesitated when she caught a glimpse of her reflection in the window. "Oh, crap," she muttered. Her hair looked like it had lost a fight with a blender. She tried pushing the wild curls back into place. It would be easier to herd swine. "Useless," she said as she took another quick peek in the pseudo mirror.

She looked down at her clothes. Her faded cotton T-shirt looked like it had come right out of the bottom of the laundry basket, which it had. She pressed the palm of her hand down the front of the shirt in a failed attempt to press out the wrinkles.

No wonder Detective Salazar had looked at a loss for words when he'd first seen her. She sighed, nothing she could do now. Good-looking men never took a second glance at plain girls like her anyway. Why fuss over how she looked? She didn't care if he was drop dead good-looking and swaggered. She didn't care that his shoulders filled the doorway, or his dark eyes melted her bones. She needed to cowgirl up and go back in there. She pushed the door open.

He stood by the coffee pot, pouring the black liquid into two cups. He looked at her and smiled. "I hope you don't mind," he lifted the pot in her direction.

"Of course not, thanks for pouring." She placed the pastries on the table.

After he placed the cups on the table, he pulled out a chair for her. She caught the scent of musk and spice. It blended with the deep aroma of the coffee.

He sat across from her, closing his eyes before sipping from the steaming cup. "Umm, this is good. The hospital coffee tasted like plastic." She smiled and pushed the plate of pastries in front of him.

"What do you need to know, Detective?"

"Call me Tony," he said after taking a swallow of coffee. "I'd like you to describe everything. From the first scream you heard until the police arrived in the alley."

Interlocking her fingers in her lap, she thought back to the dreadful events of the night. In the chaos, she had almost forgotten the break-in. "I came downstairs because of a noise I heard in the kitchen. It was just before midnight. At first, I thought it was Tighe coming to work. He never shows up until midnight or later. My clock always shows later."

Tony stopped writing and looked up at her. She wasn't sure if it was because of his exhale or his shoulders drooping, but for a second, he looked exasperated. "I hope you are going to tell me Tighe came to work early?"

"No. I found the back door open and the tray cart toppled over, but there wasn't anyone in the kitchen." She stiffened at the recollection. "After checking nothing had been taken from the safe, I called 9-1-1."

He pulled the cup from his mouth and his eyes widened. "Did you tell any of the officers about the break-in?"

"No, the situation with the kids was so intense, I forgot all about it until after I came back here. Jimmy told me a detective would be stopping by and I didn't want to go back into the alley." A shiver ran through her at the recollection. "I thought I'd wait. It was during the first call to 9-1-1 when I heard the first scream. After the call, I looked outside and heard it again. I was pretty sure it came from the alley." She put her hands back around the mug, the heat warmed her cold fingers.

"Is tonight the first time anyone has broken into your place?"

"Yes, well, no, I'm not sure." She felt like a complete idiot. Anxiety and exhaustion clouded her memory. "I found the door open last week, around the same time. But it was so windy I just locked it and figured the wind had blown it open. Sometimes the latch doesn't catch."

"It wasn't that windy tonight."

"No, not windy enough to blow the door open like last time."

"So we have to rule that out." His tone sounded stern. He sat still for a second, but then in a softer tone he said, "Okay, I'll look into any reported break-ins around the same time and talk to patrol. I'm not sure if the two things are related, but after tonight I'm sure they'll be paying extra attention to the alley. I'll ask them to do the same here. You have my card, so call if anything, and I mean anything, is out of the ordinary." He gestured with his hand for her to continue.

"When I heard the second scream, I grabbed a flashlight and ran to the alley. I saw this guy dragging Madison. I think he was trying to drag her further into the alley. I yelled for him to stop and let go of her. I walked toward them, but I didn't know if he had a weapon, so I moved slowly. He stopped moving backwards and I stood still." She paused before lowering her voice, "I didn't want him to hurt her."

Tony stood and walked to the coffee maker. She sensed a hesitation before he turned, leaned back on the counter and gripped the edge with his hands. "You know, what you did tonight was a brave thing." His voice betrayed his disapproval. "You probably saved both those kid's lives. But you still took a dangerous risk. He could have had a gun, or gone after you."

He shook his head, grabbed the coffee pot and refilled both their cups. He sat and leaned across the table, "I don't want another person in the hospital, Keeva."

She pinched her lips and crossed her arms. Frustration began to build at the events of the evening, with herself and now with the detective. Whatever had happened tonight, the only thing she'd had control over was running into the alley. It was something she would do over in a heartbeat. She decided to ignore his comments and tell the story.

"As I was saying," she paused and looked at him to see if he had any further comments, "I couldn't see much of him since it was so dark, but I could see his features a little. He looked in my direction. It was eerie." Keeva probed her mind, trying to remember any more details, none emerged. "Then he pushed Madison. I focused on her when she ran toward me."

Lifting the cup, she lowered it without drinking. "By the time I looked up again he was almost at the other end of the alley. As I said earlier, Madison kept screaming about Todd and crying. When she pointed at Todd, I ran to him."

Tony wrote a few things in his notepad, and they finished their coffee. He stood and pulled keys from his pocket. She felt like he was stalling. Maybe he didn't want to go out in the cold.

"Is your car in the parking lot?" she asked.

"No, it's across the street."

"I can let you out the front door, it's a bit closer."

She pulled the key from her pocket and walked over, unlocked the door and pushed it open for him. Tony stopped next to her. Acutely aware of the close proximity of his body, her legs became rubbery. Shit, she was in such trouble around this man. Doing all she could not to stare at his face gave her two alternatives: to stare at his chest or to turn away. The latter was not an option and she felt like a fool staring at his chest. "Should I call if I remember anything?" she asked before realizing he'd already said that. What a moron. She bit her lower lip and peeked up at him, maybe he hadn't noticed her stupidity.

The smoothest smile she had ever seen crossed his face, and his black eyes crinkled at the corners. The moonlight through the door highlighted their glint.

"Maybe you should just call." He winked and walked out the door.

*

Still smiling when he entered the cold car, Tony barely registered the chilled leather seat. He already missed the warmth inside the café. No, he missed the warmth of Keeva. A rumble, like a volcano erupting, had risen in him and a deepening urge to stay with her had grown the longer he had sat in the café.

Pressing his head against the car seat, he closed his eyes. "Get a grip. She's just a woman like any other." No sooner had the words slipped from his mouth than his conscience pricked him telling him he was a liar. She was not like any other woman. Tonight she had run into a darkened alley, chasing off a lunatic to save Madison and Todd. Add calm, cool and beautiful to brave, she added up to be one special lady.

He sighed. He still had a job to do. He opened his laptop and found the message with Mac Ryan's address. He figured Keeva would call to warn her brother if she knew he was going to interview Mac, so he had held back the information. A tinge of guilt crept through him, and he suddenly felt sorry for the deception. He pushed back an urge to run back and tell her the truth and was surprised at his sudden remorse. Lying to catch the bad guys was a norm for him and he had never felt guilty before.

Several minutes later, he walked through the maze

of two-story apartments. His flashlight lighting the walkway, he found the apartment marked *115* and pressed the bell.

Pressing the bell a second time, he stepped back to wait. The apartments sat on the edge of town, allowing Tony a nice view of the vast sky dotted with hundreds of stars. He rang the bell again. He heard a bang, followed by a few muffled curses, and then the door cracked open. A man appeared at the door wearing only a pair of jeans. His hair, though shorter, stuck out in the same wild curls as Keeva's.

Tony held up his I.D. "Are you Mac Ryan?"

Mac leaned out the door to read the ID. "Yeah. What do you want?"

"I have a few questions to ask you. Is it okay if I come in?" Tony placed his I.D in his pocket.

Mac blinked his eyes in rapid succession and shook his head, as though trying to wake up a bit more. "Is Keeva okay? What happened?"

"A couple of teenagers were attacked tonight, and you were seen jogging in the area. I'm talking to anyone who might have seen anything."

Mac hesitated and this time stared at Tony, unblinking. "Why are you bothering me? I didn't see anyone." He started to push the door shut but Tony stopped it with his foot.

"Let me make this clear," Tony had expected the resistance but it irritated him just the same, "this isn't a pick-and-choose scenario." He placed his hand on the edge of the door, pushing it open a little more. "If you want to make it difficult, I can always make you a person of interest. Then you get to have this conversation at the station."

They both stood there staring. Tony hoped Mac would become cooperative. Then he saw Mac's facial muscles relax and heard him release a breath. Tony loosened his grip on the door.

Mac stepped back, giving Tony room to step in. He cleared some clothes and threw them on the couch, motioning for Tony to sit in the place he cleared. He plopped himself opposite Tony. The place looked like any single man's apartment, furniture not too new, a pizza box with a few old slices in it, laying open on the coffee table. There was an empty beer bottle and several empty soda cans scattered on the same table.

He pulled out the pictures of Madison and Todd, placing them on the table in front of Mac. He watched him look, tilt his head, and then he could see the recognition. Okay, time for truth or dare.

"Yeah, I have seen them before, but not tonight." He handed the pictures back to Tony. "Were they attacked at the Guardian?"

"You mean the old fire tower that looks over downtown?"

Mac nodded.

Tony considered Mac's revelation and the

Guardian's close proximity to the attack. "No, it was a few blocks away. Why do you mention it?"

"A few nights ago I was doing sprints up Cruse Avenue and decided to push myself and sprinted up the hill to the Guardian, and they were up there." Mac rubbed his hands together.

Tony noted the nervous action and it triggered new concerns. Mac had recognized them quickly. It would have been dark at the Guardian at night and he would not have had a good look at them. Had he seen them other times? Tony wondered how often and why they'd been out so late.

"Like I was saying, these kids were attacked. The boy brutally, and we believe, if he hadn't been stopped, the girl would have been next."

Mac lifted his shoulders and splayed his hands, "Why would anyone attack a couple of kids?" Mac's eyes searched Tony's for an answer.

A hollowness filled Tony's stomach. There was no good answer for what had happened to Todd. "Maybe if we knew *why*, we might be able to figure out who did it. What were Todd and Madison, that's their names, by the way, what were they doing when you saw them at the Guardian?"

"When I first saw them they were pretty hot and heavy, but became scared shitless when they saw me. I told them they'd better go since it was kind of late for them to be out." Mac shifted on the couch. "I left and figured they left a few minutes after me."

Tony crossed an ankle over his knee and sat up straighter. The lack of sleep and the lumpy chair had begun to take their toll on him and he missed the comfortable bed he had vacated over three hours ago. The non-stop investigating of a violent crime often pushed the detectives to exhaustion, and he disliked not being on his A-game. He sucked in a breath reviving himself. "What time were you out last night?

Mac closed his eyes, moving his head back and forth as though doing mental calculations and then he looked at Tony, "I can't tell you what time I left, but I know I got home around 11:30 to 11:45. I'm guessing I was out running about two hours."

Granted, Mac's timeline didn't match the attack, but he could be lying. "Anyone see you come home?"

"Yes, my neighbor, she's a nurse and just got home from her shift. We waved, she went inside and I stood outside stretching for a few minutes."

With the apartment only a few blocks away, would he have had time to run back out? Keeva would have recognized her own brother. Still, he needed facts and right now he had none. Tony would check with the neighbor, but now he was beginning to feel like Jimmy had sent him on a wild goose chase. The idiot.

"Why were you out so late?"

Tony didn't know if Mac would be of help, but

he was trying to put the pieces of a thousand-piece puzzle together, and he felt like he had too many missing ones. He had a crime that appeared senseless, witnesses unable to describe the perpetrator, and his only suspect, appeared innocent. Each piece he could gather had the potential to bring him closer to solving the puzzle.

Mac kept his focus on the floor, but began speaking. "I run to the V.A. Cemetery."

"Come again?" Tony asked. The response surprised him. Why would someone run to a cemetery in the middle of the night?

"It's just where I go." Mac flopped forward, his elbows on his knees and his head down. After a moment, he lifted his head and even though the room had little light, Tony could see Mac's eyes were damp. Mac took in a deep breath and exhaled. "The V.A. counselors told me to find a hobby, you know, something to do when I can't sleep. The problem is the only thing I can do right now is run."

"And you run to the V.A.? That's quite a jog from here for that time of night."

"I don't know where else to go. Besides someone I lost is buried there, and I go to see him." He dropped his head again and placed both hands across the back of his head.

Until now Mac's name hadn't meant anything to Tony, but he began to piece together things he remembered. About six months ago, the local paper had run an article about several local Marines stationed together in Afghanistan. An Improvised Explosive Device killed one of them. The picture under the headline had shown another Marine, in full dress, saluting over a grave. Mac had been that Marine. "The cemetery." He stroked the bristles on his chin with his forefinger and thumb. "Wasn't your friend killed in Afghanistan?" Tony knew the extremes PTSD drove people to, but now he wondered how far it drove Mac.

"That's history and I don't want to talk about it. What else do you need?" He sounded weary. "I'm tired and you interrupted one of the few nights of sleep I've had in a long time." Mac lifted his head and pushed his fingers through the rebellious curls. "Enough about my sorry life." His voice sounded steadier.

Tony took his cue and continued, "Like I was saying, those kids were attacked, the boy brutally. If you saw anything, now is the time to tell me."

"How are they?" Mac asked.

Tony let his question drop. He knew what he needed to know, for now. "Todd is being flown to Denver. He has some type of head trauma. Madison is fine, hysterical but not harmed thanks to your sister."

"Keeva?" Mac pushed himself up a little straighter. "What does she have to do with this?"

"She was working and heard Madison screaming.

She ran into the alley across from her café to help Madison, and the guy ran off."

Mac's face blanched. "What the hell was she thinking? He could've hurt her."

Tony admired Mac's protective instinct. He had the same relationship with his own sister. "I told her the same thing, but she's okay. Keeva is the only witness we have besides Todd and Madison." Drawing in a deep breath, he continued, "Madison is not able to remember much right now, and Todd is in a coma, so…"

Mac shook his head, "Damn her, she doesn't think. I can't believe she just ran into the alley." His eyes widened. "Wait, you don't think I had anything to do with hurting Todd and Madison, do you?" The creases that formed between Mac's eyes expressed his annoyance. "Is that why you're really here?"

Tony shook his head. "I need to know what you saw last night. I don't know who hurt those kids though I intend to find out." Mac's behavior concerned him, but he doubted he committed a crime, at worst he had witnessed one. "If that means questioning everyone and anyone who could have seen something, I will."

Mac lifted his head slightly off his hands, "Who told you they saw me running?"

Tony placed both feet on the floor and leaned forward. The evidence didn't prove if the kids were targeted or attacked at random. Since people were creatures of habit, he doubted this had been the first time the attacker had been in the alley late at night. Maybe Mac had seen more than he realized on one of his runs. "From one of our officers," he paused, "Jimmy Smith." Tony saw the muscles in Mac's jaw tense in response to the name. He wondered what history the men shared.

"I didn't see anything unusual." Mac rubbed one arm with the other hand. "I knew Jimmy in high school and he's always been an ass. But why would he think I wouldn't call the police if I saw something suspicious?"

Tony suddenly liked Mac a little better. Anyone who shared his opinion of Smith was a good enough guy, and he smiled at Mac's comment. "How about telling me what you saw, or didn't see and I'll decide what is relevant and what isn't?"

"Damn it. That's just it. I didn't see or do anything." He balled his fists and closed his eyes for a moment. "The run to the VA is just short of ten miles. I add a few blocks to round it out and tonight I ran up to Last Chance Gulch and around the café. I saw Keeva's light on upstairs." He leaned back on the couch. "She gets pissed and gives me grief when I run late at night so I just headed back without stopping there. I saw Jimmy right before I turned down Last

Chance Gulch. He was parked on the corner of Last Chance and 12th Avenue."

Tony rested his elbows on his knees and clasped his hands together. He wanted Mac to continue focusing on the teens and any encounters he might have had with them. "When I showed you those pictures, how did you recognize Todd and Madison if you only saw them for a few minutes in the dark?"

"I never said that was the only time I saw them." Mac stood and walked over to the refrigerator, pulling out two bottles of water. "When I mentioned the fire tower, you asked about seeing them there. I met them once before and talked to them a bit. Mostly Todd, but it was Madison who started it all."

A sense of elation lifted Tony and he felt his instincts about Mac's knowledge would pay off. "Do you remember what day and around what time you first saw them? And where?" Tony stopped himself from asking too many questions so Mac could process the ones he asked.

Mac held the door open as though thinking. The two water bottles dangled from one hand, the refrigerator still open. "Oh, shit, Madison must have been right." The refrigerator door inched to a close when Mac let it go and moved away.

Mac handed Tony a bottle of water and stepped back to lean against the apartment's small kitchen counter. "I saw them a few weeks back. They were turning off Helena Avenue, near Jackson Street." His voice lowered. "Crap, I can't believe this is happening."

Something in the way Mac lowered his voice, as though ready to reveal something new, lessened a piece of Tony's tension. The pressure that had gripped his muscles all night began to loosen. "Mac, if you know something, now is the time to talk." Lifting the dew-covered bottle, he swallowed some of the cold water.

"I didn't think much of it at the time, but Madison thought someone had followed them." Mac shook his head and blew out a breath. "About two weeks ago," he paused, "I was jogging down Helena Avenue, adding in the few extra blocks. I saw them walking when they stopped me." He tapped the bottle against his chin and a red mark grew against his pale skin. "Well, Madison stopped me. Todd kept telling her to let it go. At that time I had never seen them before, and at first worried they were up to no good." He stilled. "But Madison seemed pretty scared. She said she thought some guy was following them. Todd insisted he hadn't seen anyone and that she was just nervous."

Stepping back to the chair, Mac folded his long frame into the low chair. Tony admired the younger man's agility. "Man, this is awful." He continued. "She asked me to stand and wait until Todd walked her to the door, then she wanted me to stay with Todd." He shrugged. "You could tell he was embarrassed. I told him it was fine and that I could use some company for the end of the run, so I waited."

Tony read Mac's sincerity, but something about Madison stopping a stranger didn't fit. Speaking to a different stranger because she was afraid of one stranger didn't make sense. "Why you? For all they knew you were the one who had followed them?"

Mac nodded. "When Madison stopped me she asked if I was 'the marine' from the paper. I had just run under a street light and I guess she recognized me."

He shifted, looking uncomfortable at the reminder and Tony guessed there was more than notoriety that bothered Mac about the article.

"When Todd got back he said he didn't need a babysitter." He shrugged. "Who can blame him? I'd have balked, too. I reassured him about having some company. He said he lived in Reeders Village. I had to go that far and was able to convince him I was chill with it."

Tony waited while Mac paused, noticing how he took his time just like Keeva. They were similar not just in looks but in other ways. They kept the same odd hours and because of that habit, they were both involved in this mess. Thoughts of Keeva sent a warm rush through him. "Did you see anyone while you accompanied Todd?"

"No, that's just it, I didn't see anyone around."

His wide-eyed expression looked disbelieving at Tony. "Hell, I may be a Marine, but I'm not an ass. If I saw anybody who could have been a problem, I'd have called the cops." He took a swallow of water. "Todd told me he didn't think anyone had been following them. so I figured Madison imagined it." Mac set his now-empty water bottle on the table. "Damn. I asked why he didn't drive her home, or have his parents drive her and he said his parents didn't care for Madison. They thought she was a bit wild for him, so he never told them he was with her. He'd wait until they went to bed and sneak out to meet her on the corner where she stopped me."

Mac's fingers intertwined, and he placed them palms out against his forehead. "God, I wish I would have knocked and woke them up."

Tony felt sorry for Mac. Seems like he had enough troubles without the guilt of what had happened tonight. "Don't beat yourself up. I think his parents ignored Todd's behavior. It was their job to watch their son, not yours." He moved to the edge of the chair. "He seems to be the golden kid that could do no wrong. His father told me he knew Todd was sneaking out. He thought it was the boys out partying." Tony knew his own father would have knocked him into next Sunday if he'd caught him sneaking out. But he met quite a few fathers who thought it okay for their sons to break a few rules. "He said boys will be boys." Tony rested his forearms across his legs.

"I forgot all about Madison's concern. It didn't even ping the radar until I began thinking about the night I met them." Mac's words slid out in a monotone.

Mac clenched his head with his interlaced hands. "Man, this is so fucked up. When I saw them again, I just told them to leave the fire tower. God, I wish I'd done more."

"You helped. Now I can work with the idea someone might have targeted Todd and Madison specifically. I'll talk to Madison and Keeva again tomorrow and see if they can recall more details."

Pushing himself up to his feet, Tony stretched. It felt good to move. "Your information gave me a lot to work with. If you saw them, so did someone else. Even if Madison can't remember much about last night, I bet she'll remember what spooked her some of the previous nights." Tony walked to the door and grabbed the handle. He turned back to Mac. "Sorry to have woken you. If you remember anything, call me no matter what the time."

CHAPTER 3

NERVOUS ENERGY HAD kept Keeva going until mid-morning when lack of sleep and tiredness took over. Her muscles felt limp and no amount of coffee kept her eye lids open. Her mind had long since disconnected from the bustling café. The story of the previous night's attack had spread in the small city and had attracted the curious. Most were looking for bits of gossip after having heard rumors connecting the café to the crime. She avoided mentioning her involvement with the attack to her staff, allowing them plausible deniability.

Keeva pushed aside the thought of calling a cab to get home when Mac stepped through the café's kitchen door. "Oh, am I glad to see you. I'm exhausted and need a ride home." She professed as she dragged a stool from under the work counter and dropped onto it.

"You okay?" Mac wrapped his arms around her, pulling her into a tight hug. Gratitude for her brother's support surged through her.

Keeva pulled back and looked up at Mac. He felt so thin. She wondered if he had lost even more weight since his return from Afghanistan.

Mac's hair, a shorter version of hers, fell in curls around his face and his lips lifted to a grin. The twinkle in his hazel eyes matched his upbeat mood. An instant rush of relief washed through her. The world felt right when Mac smiled at her. He looked just like their mother when he smiled.

Her mother. She swallowed the painful memory. The moment of contentment washed away and her roller coaster emotions screeched to a halt. Right now, she had to focus on life at this moment, not the past.

"Did the police talk to you?" She asked and pulled away from him.

"A detective stopped by and woke me up at 3 a.m. Jimmy Smith said he saw me out running the same time the kids were hurt."

Needing something to distract her from the memory of the night before she stood, grabbing some pans that were drying in the industrial dishwasher and put them up on the shelf. "Where you running around here?"

"Yes, and no, I didn't lose it and hurt those kids." He sounded annoyed. "Don't worry sis, I'm not that crazy. Yet." He playfully punched her shoulder, but the spark in his eyes disappeared.

"Don't call yourself that, and I'm not accusing you. I know you'd never hurt anyone."

She shook her head. How could he think that had been her concern? Thankful as she was he had come home without any physical injuries, she still knew the mental and emotional toll PTSD had taken on him. The problem of how others saw him did bother her. Some of his friends spoke to her about his isolation and worried for him. But others avoided him and treated him like a leper. In the café, she had overheard two of his former friends say he had come back weird. Keeva had wanted to scream at them, but she had known it wouldn't do any good. Jimmy, surprisingly, had been one of the few people that had called her aside and offered to help. She hoped his sincerity had been real. Too tired to think it through, she decided to let the subject drop.

"Anyway, why would they think I wouldn't have recognized you?"

"I think it's just Jimmy. He still acts as though we're in high school and he's the hall monitor. Don't worry, what's he proving? That I'm a bat shit, crazy vet? Hell, that's old news." He jumped up to sit on the counter, his long legs dangling almost to the floor.

"And what were you thinking running into that situation? Do you have any idea how dangerous it was?"

"You sound like Tony. He said the same thing."

"*Tony*? His eyes widened, the light in them returning when he chuckled. "You're on a first name basis?" He arched an eyebrow. "Does my little sister have a crush on the big bad detective?"

Keeva felt heat rise up her cheeks. Turning her back to him, she hung her apron on a hook. "He told me to call him Tony, so stop teasing."

He grabbed a pastry from the cooling rack and jabbed it in her direction. "Never, it's my life mission to tease you. Anyway, he probably has a black book full of girlfriends."

"Don't be an idiot. I am not interested in him. Just drive me home without the wise cracks. I'm exhausted and left my car home. I slept here last night, or rather, hardly slept, after all the drama." No money to pay the insurance premium meant her car stayed in her garage, a small bit of information Mac didn't need to know.

"Ha, and you give me a hard time about running in the middle of the night. You're the one who jogs to work at *o-dark-ugly*. And let's not forget running right into an attack in that alley."

"Oh, please. You'd have done the same, Mr. Macho Marine." She giggled at their bantering. It felt

46

good to put her attention on something other than the previous night's gruesome events.

"By the way, I saw Henry yesterday. He says you run funny hours." She rested against the counter next to Mac.

"I swear that crazy old man is following me."

"He's not following you. And don't call him crazy, he's," she tried to think of a nice way to describe the eccentric man, "just a little different."

Mac rolled his eyes. "That's an understatement."

"Betty and Nana looked after him like a brother," she reminded him. "With Nana dead, and Betty in the senior citizens apartments, he's a lost soul and keeping an eye on us makes him feel important."

"It's not normal to be watching grown people and reporting all their actions like we live in a police state." He bit the pastry he held.

"He doesn't report anything, and who would he report it to?" She stifled a giggle. "He just watches us and makes sure we're okay. And right now he doesn't think you," she poked a finger at him, "are okay. So he tells me." Her laugh escaped when Mac made a fake attempt to bite her finger.

Keeva grabbed her purse from a cupboard. "And you owe me for a couple dozen pastries."

He grinned, finishing off the pastry before grabbing a second one.

She spied the basement door open and the light

on downstairs. All the employees were out front working or in the kitchen where she could see them. So who was down there? A feeling of déjà vu overwhelmed Keeva and the hairs on the back of her neck stood up. The memory of the knocked-over tray rack from last night made her wonder if someone had broken in again. She pushed her concern aside. No one would break in with everyone here. Lucy had probably forgotten to lock the door to the basement. She held up a finger, a signal to Mac she would need a minute.

The ceiling dropped lower at the last step, forcing Keeva to duck before entering the basement. She stopped short at the last step where a large stack of newly delivered boxes blocked her way. The number of boxes stunned her. The café rarely placed orders this large. Pulling out several packing slips so she could view the contents without opening the boxes, she was surprised to see the slip listed expensive cake pans and decorating equipment. To her further surprise, behind all the boxes was a brand new industrial mixer. It had to be a mistake. The two-year-old café didn't need new equipment.

Not wanting anyone to open the boxes before she looked into it, Keeva decided to put all of it in the locked storage closet for now. While she was padlocking the door, Mac called down the narrow stairs telling her he would be in the car waiting.

Returning upstairs, she locked the door behind her, replacing the basement key and pocketing the padlock key in her purse. Lucy was pulling some cookies from the oven. "Luce, there is a large order downstairs. Do you know anything about it?"

Lucy, stretching to place a tray of cookies in the top level of the baking rack, stilled before turning to Keeva. "I thought you placed the order." Lucy's brows furrowed over her eyes. "They were delivered during this morning's rush. If you didn't, and I didn't, then who did?"

"It must be a mistake then." Keeva shook her head. Her weariness made it difficult to concentrate. She really needed sleep right now and not to have to tackle someone else's screw up. "I locked them in the closet so no one opens anything. I'll take care of it tomorrow. Mac's waiting and I need to go home and get some sleep."

*

The street lamp illuminated the white clouds made by her warm breaths as Keeva jogged to the café the following morning. The weather station had revealed it was a chilly twenty-two degrees when she'd left her apartment, but the computer had promised her a warm sunny day in the high forties. The springtime weather for southwestern Montana could be schizo-phrenic in its unpredictability.

She jogged up Last Chance Gulch, slowing to a

walk when she reached the back of her building. She peered around the building to the alley and suppressed the urge to hurry inside as she remembered the horrific scene she had run into two nights ago. She'd called a friend who worked at the hospital and had learned Madison had gone home and that Todd had been stabilized and transferred to a large city hospital. A cold chill spiraled down her spine and she shivered.

Something tapped her shoulder and Keeva jumped, drawing in a startled breath. She turned to see Henry, an oversized coat hanging from his wiry frame and wavy grey hair escaping from his stocking cap. She let out a relief filled breath. "You scared me Henry."

"Sorry, Mizz Keeva, I didn't mean to." He lowered his head and pushed his hands into his pockets.

Keeva felt a pang of guilt for having snapped at him. "It's okay, I'm just a little jumpy after," she hesitated, not sure how much to tell Henry, "after those teenagers got hurt. You should be careful, too. You shouldn't be wandering around in the dark. I don't think they found the man yet."

"It's okay, Mizz Keeva. I know who that man is. But I don't go near him."

Henry' few attempts at conversation, bordered on strange on a good day. Mildly schizophrenic and a little paranoid, he functioned well enough, though his rare conversations were like trying to understand a foreign language. She had known him since childhood and still had trouble comprehending his jumbled communication. But she tried to understand him; she owed him that much.

Two years ago, on the eve of the café's grand opening, Keeva had stood alone facing the café and contemplating the future. All the hope and happiness that should have lay ahead of her, had been muffled by a deep, empty ache. Though close to her mother through most of her years, they had begun to fight over what her mother had perceived as Keeva's lack of goals after graduating college. Keeva had worked part-time temporary jobs since graduation but had refused offers to make them permanent. Her mother had encouraged and cajoled Keeva to find full-time employment. But she had wanted satisfaction, not just a job. Her mother's mantra: You worked because you needed to, not because you wanted to.

After one long and heated argument on the matter, Keeva's parents had gone out for a drive. The words she had yelled at her parents that day had been the last she had ever spoken to them. With pain in her heart, like a diploma from hell, she'd set out to make them proud. Taking her half of the inheritance, she'd turned her grandmother's house into the café, working twelve to fifteen hour days to open in six months.

On the cool night before the grand opening, she'd stood in front of the cafe, aware for the first time that no matter how successful the cafe would become it wouldn't assuage the guilt that lived deep in her soul. Believing she had been standing alone, mustering her inner strength to face the future, she had felt a tranquil presence. Henry. He had not said a word, he'd just stood there alongside her. She didn't know how long they had stood together but it must have been quite a while. And in that act, Henry had offered her the comfort and support she'd needed to move forward.

She had always thought Henry to be crazy, often reminding Betty and her grandmother of her opinion. But that day, she'd known, somewhere under his quirky speech, somewhere buried in his delusions, resided a caring and insightful soul. Since then, he had remained endeared to her.

Henry shifted his weight, crunching the gravel of the parking lot under his worn sneakers. The noise, conspicuous in the quiet dawn, drew Keeva's focus back to him. "You saw him? How do you know who he is?"

"I was under the bridge by the railroad. Then the police told me to go, so I hid on the side of Mizz Barbara's 's house. Well, it's yours now."

Keeva suppressed the urge to rush him along knowing it would rattle him and then he would never get to the point. "And when did you see him, Henry? How did you know it was him?" Though she spoke quietly and calmly, she didn't feel calm. Keeva edged closer in order to hear him better.

"It had to be him, like the cougars that hide in the mountains stalking their kill, hiding. I saw him in the dark. By that tree." He pointed a crooked, arthritic finger toward the alley.

A cold shiver ran down Keeva's back. Would he come back? Her heart skipped a beat, because something told her Henry was telling the truth.

"Did he stand in the alley?" Dawn's light made it easier for her to see his lined face before he looked at the ground and kicked the dirt with his tattered tennis shoe. She worried he would forget the details. "It's important you tell me anything you saw." She sucked in a quick short breath, holding it in anticipation.

As though reading her thoughts, he looked up at her eyes. She put a reassuring hand on his arm and smiled. Letting her breath out slowly, she tried to convey comfort to Henry with a smile of support. Though his state of mind could be precarious at times, he still might be the one connection they had to finding the attacker.

"I won't get in trouble, will I, Mizz Keeva? Will the police be after me for seeing him?" His eyes searched hers, like a lost child looking for help locating a missing parent.

She read the fear in his eyes and felt a stab of guilt for causing him any distress. "No, you won't get in trouble. You didn't do anything wrong so the police won't be after you. But if it is the same man who hurt those kids, it might help the police." She bit her lower lip. His eyes remained focused on her face, and she wondered whether he was thinking, or was confused.

A sudden smile put a twinkle in his grey, life-worn eyes. "First, he was in the alley." He pointed. "Then, over there." His arm moved, pointing away from the alley's entrance. "By that tree. The moon was big so I saw real well."

He shuffled his feet some more. "After the police hollered, I walked here. Always before, it was safe here. But with that man hurting those kids, it don't feel safe no more." Keeva knew he was right. Something had changed two nights ago. He placed his clenched hands on the sides of his head and his shuffling intensified to a side step. "I prayed for them. Do you think it will help them, Mizz Keeva?"

The expression of faith surprised her. "Yes, I do believe prayers will help." She paused to consider how to phrase her question, knowing how easily the wrong words could unnerve him. "Could you see if the man wore a coat, a hat, anything?" She doubted he could have seen much in the dark, but hoped for a little something. She rubbed her arms as the chill seeped through her windbreaker to her damp running shirt.

"No, I don't see real good in the night." The exaggerated movements continued a few more seconds, and then he suddenly stilled. His face brightened and his mouth parted. "I remembered." He beamed, not saying another word.

"You remembered what, Henry?"

"He had on a Unabomber shirt." He stood, as proud as if he'd just won a prize for knowing the answer.

For a brief second, dread passed through her. Could he be confusing another event with this situation? "I'm not sure what you mean."

He widened his eyes, looking at her as though she were the one behaving oddly. "You know, one with the hood?" He tapped the top of his head.

"A hoodie?"

Henry nodded. "Yes, a hoodie."

Unlike her childhood nightmares of ghosts chasing her, fears which never materialized, this nightmare had just become real. "Did you see the color?" She felt light headed and placed her hand on the building to steady herself.

"Dark, real dark, like at night. Did I do good?"

"You did great." Steadying herself, she faced Henry. Knowing what the attacker was capable of doing, she now worried for him. "Please don't walk around at night anymore. It isn't safe." She opened the door, but turned at the sudden memory of her conversation with Betty. "Betty asked about you. She would like to see you and asked if I would drive you over to The Crossroads Apartments."

"I'd like that, Mizz Keeva. We'd sit here on the porch with your granma, Mizz Barbara, and talk about Capital City when it used to be our day." He stared into the distance as though recalling some distant memory.

"Do you want coffee, Henry? It will take me a few minutes to make it, and I can get the rolls for you."

"No, thank you, Mizz Keeva. I'll just take the rolls and go."

She unlocked the cafe and stepped inside. Each day, at her request, Tighe left a chain of bags on the counter near the back door. Henry's was the largest of the group.

"Here you go, Henry. It's always nice to see you." She handed Henry his rolls. "Stop in later in the day and let me know when I can take you to see Betty."

"Okay, Mizz Keeva."

Keeva's heart tugged as she watched Henry limp away. He blended into the quiet darkness.

*

After changing, she returned to the kitchen and picked up the stack of sticky notes. "Tighe's daily litany of complaints" she called them. The first, he chastised her once again, for *supporting the city's freeloaders*, which he claimed would cost her the business. In truth, she suspected he only worried about losing his job and didn't care at all if she lost her business.

Next, a complaint about the cleaning crew and a phone number for his girlfriend who could do a better job. "Right, she also costs twice as much," she said to the little yellow note. She crumbled them all, flinging them into the center of the trash bin.

None of the other employees were due in until six, leaving Keeva a few minutes alone. Ripples, like a tickle ran through her stomach. She had to call Tony. She needed to tell him about Henry, and she wanted to see his face and know he understood the precariousness of the situation.

The anticipation of speaking to him, let alone seeing him, made her stomach flip.

"Loh," the voice sounded half asleep.

She hesitated, her mouth felt dry. "Hi, Detective, it's Keeva Ryan." The phone got quiet and she heard a thump.

"*Carajo!*" The word sounded distant, followed by some fumbling. "Keeva?" he said into the phone.

He didn't elaborate, so she continued. "Yes. I'm sorry to wake you, but I need to talk to you."

"Um, now?" He sounded a bit more awake.

"Yes. I'll be very busy later and won't have time to talk. This is the only time that works for me." She bit a fingernail. Staring toward the back door she saw a bright piece of yellow paper on the floor.

Keeva picked up the scrap. Ignoring the writing, she walked to the trash to drop it in as Tony responded, "It'll take me about half an hour."

"A half hour at the café is fine." She pocketed her phone and let the paper fall into the trash bin.

As the paper floated into the bin, she spotted a crude drawing of stick figures on the reverse side. One of the figures had a riot of curls with tendrils sticking out. It struck her that the drawing resembled her. Curious, she picked the paper up, flattening out the wrinkles, expecting to find a comical picture made by an employee. She was wrong.

The drawing was of a male-looking stick figure and the curly haired figure touching, as though holding hands. Her breath cut off at the sight of the third figure. The prone figure had dark lines snaking from the head. Was it meant to be blood? As though wafting off the paper, the memory of the smell of Todd's blood returned. Her stomach roiled.

She flipped the paper over. In bold letters, were the words:

I see you, you see me

we are one

you are mine, only mine

mine or die

my brave and pretty Keeva

She swallowed the bile that had risen in her throat. Who would write this? From its location on the floor, just to the side of the door, it must have been in the door jam. It had probably blown in when she'd opened the door.

The twisted words and drawing seemed to jump off the page, as though it was a viper ready to attack. Her focus was so intent, on the horror of the bizarre note, she didn't hear Lucy open the back door.

"Keeva, are you all right?" Lucy dropped her purse on the counter and walked over to Keeva. Looking over her shoulder, she pulled the paper from Keeva's hand. "Oh, my God. Where did you get this?" She held the paper up, shaking it in front of Keeva.

Keeva pulled back in fear, the poisonous intention had hit its mark. "I don't know." Her voice was raspy. The words didn't want to come out. "It was on the floor. I think someone put it in the door, and when I opened the door it blew in."

"You need to call the police. I'll make us some tea."

"The detective is already on his way here."

*

The café felt familiar to Tony the second time he walked through it. Something savory mingled with the sweet and yeasty aromas.

Anticipation propelling him, Tony took the stairs

two at a time. Stopping at the top of the stairs, he took a moment to take a breath before…before what?

Nothing rattled him. Ever.

During covert ops with Delta, he'd walked into nests of Al-Qaeda, knowing he would die a slow painful death if they discovered his identity. He had always kept his calm. As a CIA agent, ruthless warlords in Chechnya's back alleys had never caused him to twitch. The bigger the challenge, the steadier he had held his nerves. Until now.

Now he stood like a nervous teenager, sweat dripping down his neck as he tried to steady his shaking hands before seeing Keeva. He moved toward the room she used as an office.

This time she was sitting at her desk when he walked in. Her hands rubbed her thighs, as though she was trying to get rid of something distasteful off her hands. She stared at a crumpled piece of paper.

He opened his mouth, and then shut it. Like a mindless jellyfish, he couldn't find a word to say. "Keeva?"

She focused her eyes on him. Her face was paler than two nights ago and the dark purple smudges under her eyes had deepened. Someone else had caused Todd's injuries and he loathed seeing her tormented. Tormented but still captivating.

She smiled up at him. "Hello, Tony, thanks for coming so early." She sounded apprehensive. He knew cops made people nervous, but he had thought they had shared something different and had moved beyond the typical nervousness related to his occupation. It disappointed him that they hadn't. She took a quick glance at the paper, and her smile disappeared.

"It's not a problem." He stepped into the room.

Keeva held her hand out toward an open chair, "Please, sit."

In one motion, he pulled the chair closer to her and dropped into it. She took another glance at the paper. What in the hell could it be? He tried to make out what was on the paper but all he could see were bent stick figures.

"I'm not sure where to begin."

"Start with why you called me this morning," he suggested. Something in Keeva's demeanor had changed since the night of the attack. When he'd first met her, she'd appeared almost stoic. Now she looked as though someone or something had sucked the life from her. He suspected that the small piece of yellow paper was the culprit.

She told him about talking to Henry, an old friend of the family. She said Henry was a little off, but she believed he'd seen the attacker hanging around near the alley. It sounded like Henry had confirmed much of what Mac had said. But something in the way she spoke, the softness of her voice, the hesitation and constant side glances at the paper told Tony much more than she revealed by her words alone. Someone or something had upset her and it made him angry.

"I'll need an address or phone number to take a statement from him." He reached into his shirt pocket, taking out his cell phone. Looking at her he waited for her to recite the number.

"Henry doesn't work that way." Closing her eyes and inhaling, she hesitated before letting out a long, slow breath and looking at him. "I know it's bizarre. If Henry even has a phone number, I don't know it. He just shows up." She held his gaze.

"I can't just take your word. I need to speak to him."

She sighed. "I know. But Henry will clam up if you take him down to the police station. He's paranoid and schizophrenic. If you approach him he'll freak."

He wanted to dig more into Henry, but she picked up the paper and began fiddling with it, bending it back and forth. Afraid she might rip it before he could see it he slid the phone back into his pocket and placed one hand over her fingers then with the other, gently removed the paper. As he unfolded the paper and read the threatening words, anger welled up in him. Pressure built in his chest. Flipping it over, he saw the drawing. "*Ay, Dios mío,*" he whispered.

"Where did you get this?" This changed things. Up until now, they had considered the attack an isolated incident but now it was clear, someone was threatening

Keeva. He wanted to beat the shit out of the asshole who had written this.

"I found it on the floor downstairs. I think it might have been stuck in the door jam. I was busy talking to Henry and didn't notice it." Tony could see the vein in her neck pulse.

Henry sounded a few dominoes short of a game, and he had been at the café earlier. "Do you think Henry could have put it there?"

She furrowed her brow. "No, Henry would never do anything like that. He looks out for Mac and me by stopping by here or walking near Mac's apartment. We've known him forever. Yeah, he's a bit different, but he'd never threaten anyone."

Different? Tony thought unhinged would be a better description, but he kept the thought to himself.

"No, never." Keeva shook her head.

Tony pulled an evidence bag from inside his jacket pocket and placed the paper inside. He had an early meeting with the Chief of Police but detested the idea of leaving Keeva alone.

"How do we resolve this? I need to interview him?"

She pinched her lips, and then looked at her phone, opening the calendar. "I can see if I can find him today, and I'll call Betty. Betty was my grandmother's closest friend. She and my grandmother always watched out for Henry. He'll cooperate if Betty is there." She tapped the phone, and he could see the calendar open to a date, filled with appointments. "I have time tomorrow or the next day. I'll work at tracking him down. If not, he'll stop by in the next day or two. He never misses more than one day. He wants to see Betty and I know he will be comfortable around her."

Tony preferred to conduct interviews at the police station, it kept him in control, but he didn't argue the arrangement. Right now he didn't have many options. "Okay, call me when you set a time."

He looked at her soft lips, suddenly wondering what they'd taste like, what they'd look like swollen with passion. He sucked in a deep breath. He needed air.

CHAPTER 4

KEEVA WISHED SHE'D finally just fixed her bike when she walked outside and realized how dark it was. She thought about calling Mac or Lucy, but they would question why she hadn't driven to work. Right now she didn't need any lectures, or reprimands for not asking them to loan her the money for car insurance.

She started a slow jog, giving her blood time to flow and warm her muscles. A tornado of thoughts about the note, the financial problems at the bakery, and Tony whirled in her head. Running always helped her relax, and as she mentally sorted through these events, she began to feel better.

Her heart beat in rhythm with her pace by the time she reached Benton Avenue. Except for the light evening traffic, there wasn't anyone else around.

The sidewalk in front of her became dark, the tall trees and dense hedges blocked out the glow from nearby lights. The memory of the dark alley sent a sense of dread rippling through her.

Her breathing accelerated. She couldn't run into the street, and the hedges prevented her from moving in another direction. She began to pick up her pace, wanting to get past the shaded area. Then twenty feet in front of her, the hedges moved and a shadow emerged. She blinked, her pace slowed. No, it couldn't be. She would have seen someone following her.

Her feet froze in place and she rubbed her eyes, wishing the sight would vanish like her childhood nightmares. It couldn't be him. But it was. She could see the same dark hoodie and he had the same silhouette she had seen running away in the alley. She began moving backwards, afraid to turn her back on him. She wanted to run back to the café, but she had always been a slow runner. She looked around frantically. The few cars that had been around were long gone and the street was deserted. She needed to call for help.

Keeva unzipped her jacket and pulled her phone from the inside pocket. She needed to call someone, but numbers wouldn't come to her. Her fingers shook as she looked at the brightly lit phone. Hurry, hurry! She punched in 9-1-1. Her thoughts jumbled. Two cars drove by. She wanted to scream and point at the man. She wondered if they saw him. She sucked to get air, and nothing happened. She felt dizzy. The phone began ringing and she bent over, her chest squeezing.

"Capital City 9-1-1, what is your emergency?"

"Um," words wouldn't come out, the sidewalk moved under her feet. She looked back at the man. Nothing. Nobody was there. Keeva blinked. A vise squeezed her throat and her heart pounded like a fist inside her chest. What had happened? He must have run back into the bushes.

"Hello, is this an emergency?"

"I'm sorry. I…" her mouth had gone dry and she had trouble speaking.

"Are you okay? Can you tell me your name?"

"I'm really sorry. I'm Keeva Ryan. I'm so embarrassed." The phone shook in her hand and as a result, she pressed it closer to her face. "I witnessed a crime the other night and I'm just spooked. I'm sorry." She wanted to stop apologizing, but the words kept coming. She stared at the spot in front of her. Had she imagined him?

"Do you need a police officer?"

"No, thank you." She whispered the last words and touched the phone, ending the call. Home. She needed to get home. Willing her feet to move, she placed one foot in front of the other. It felt like she had weights wrapped around her ankles. Her legs wobbled like a newborn fawn, unsteady with their gate. Placing the phone in her side pocket, she kept her hand wrapped tightly around it. She moved forward on shaky legs.

Like a dark tunnel inviting horrors, the shadowed sidewalk loomed in front of her. Her breaths still shallow, and her muscles tense with the fear that the man was hiding in the shrubbery. Cold sweat began soaking through her clothes while her heart exploded in her chest. Forcing her legs to keep moving, she reached the place the dark apparition had stood and stepped into the street.

She increased her pace, quickly passing the shaded spot. She glanced back, causing herself to stumble. Panic pushed her into a full sprint. A few blocks ahead, relief flooded her when she saw her street. Rounding the corner, she willed her feet to slow and a short while later, her apartment came into view.

She had just reduced her stride when a police car passed her and pulled to a stop in front of her apartment. Jimmy Smith stepped out of the car and turned to face her. She now felt like a bigger idiot than she had ten minutes ago.

She walked the last block, hoping he'd leave. "Hi Jimmy," she said as she crossed the street. Her face had already turned red from the run, but she knew her embarrassment would have caused the same reaction.

Under the street lamp, she could see him grinning. "Making crank calls these days?"

Keeva didn't find any humor in his joke. She

smirked. "I can't believe they sent you here. I told the dispatcher it was a mistake." She moved next to Jimmy and leaned her back against the car and looked up at him. He smiled but his questioning eyes remained unmoving, frozen on her.

By brandishing a bad boy attitude along with scintillating good looks and a loner personality, he had created a keep-away-from-me persona. With equanimity, Keeva had both feared and adored Jimmy, finding it safer to keep her distance until a chance conversation had revealed their shared grief over losing their parents at a young age. Their common loss had formed a bond along with a comfortable friendship. Now, like swings moving in tandem, they could chat with ease.

"Don't worry. She knew I was in the area and told me about the call. I just wanted to check you were okay." After a few seconds, he tipped his head and lifted his eyebrows. "Well?"

"I'm fine," she moaned. "I just thought I saw someone that looked like the man who attacked those kids. I panicked." She shivered, the cold air seeping through her jacket. "It's just nerves."

"You know they haven't found the guy. Are you sure you didn't see him?"

She was no longer positive what she had seen. "Honest. There wasn't anyone there. I had been running hard and mistook a shadow for a person."

He shook his head. "I can't force you to tell me

what happened, but I'm not convinced." He crossed his arms and looked ready to stand there all night if she didn't answer. "I know about the note." He eyed her, she suspected, trying to judge her reaction.

She shrugged and looked at the ground.

"There is a chance someone is following you. You need to take this seriously." He turned sideways, placing a hand over the top of the car, stepping closer to her. "Just tell me what you saw and I'll pass it on to," he paused, "Salazar." His voice sounded condescending when he said Tony's name. She wondered what Tony had done to make Jimmy dislike him.

She took a breath, not relishing the idea of reliving the embarrassing moment. "There isn't much to tell. I had been running home from work and was running hard. I guess I'm still jumpy from," she paused, "the other night. I can't be sure I saw anything. It looked like a man with a hoodie stepped out onto the sidewalk. I pulled out my phone," she still held the phone in her hand and fumbled it in her pocket. "I started to call 9-1-1, but when I looked up he wasn't there." Her cheeks heated with renewed embarrassment. "I was just nervous. I'm sorry to make such a big deal."

"You don't need to apologize, this is what I do." He put a hand on her shoulder, turning her to face him. "And you're a friend. I'd have come anyway. As a friend and a cop, I'm going to ask you to take more precautions. At least until we catch this guy. Drive your car instead of running. If you must run, find someone to run with. What if it had been him?"

"I know. I promise to be more careful when I go out." He didn't need to know being careful meant riding her bicycle not driving her car. She would still be cautious. She was broke, not stupid. "I need a favor from you too, Jimmy."

"Depends, it might cost you." He gave her a half-smile.

She rolled her eyes. "Please don't mention this to Mac if you see him?" Though Mac and Jimmy had never gotten along, it was a small town and she knew there was a chance they would see each other. "He's got enough on his plate and doesn't need to know about tonight."

"It's a deal, but you need to promise to be more cautious."

Keeva gave a mock salute. "Yes, sir."

"You sure you're all right? I can stay around, check the apartment if you like?" His icy blue eyes softened.

She could still feel the tension in her muscles and had to hug her abdomen to control the shaking. "Would you? Maybe just check the apartment?" She felt childish asking, but she didn't know how she would be able to get herself into the apartment alone right now.

Five minutes later, she watched from her window as Jimmy waved at her before driving away. She shivered, still feeling the cold chill of that dark shadow. She brushed it off. It had to be nervousness and left-over adrenaline.

*

He let the hedge fall back in place. He had to be more careful. Twice today he'd almost been caught. His description had been all over the news so he had been trying to keep a low profile. But he needed to see her as often as he could. From watching the café, he'd figured out which way she'd go when she ran home and he'd tried to follow her, almost stepping into her on the sidewalk.

At first he had wanted to talk to her, but she'd looked so afraid. He had wanted to let her know they belonged together but he'd hung back, afraid she'd scream.

He knew they were meant to be, but realized she might not have recognized the inevitability of their joining, yet. If she hadn't, and she screamed, the police would come and he'd get arrested.

Keeva had looked beautiful. The street had been quiet, so he'd parked and hid in some bushes to watch her go by. He'd seen the cop car pass and saw her stop running. When he saw Jimmy get out of the car, he had clenched his teeth against the anger that seared within him.

He felt a stab in his head. It felt like a knife had pierced his brain. He rubbed his forehead but it didn't help. As he watched Jimmy standing next to her, smiling, he had wanted to be there. Jimmy didn't deserve her. Why was Jimmy always there?

He had to get rid of him. He clenched his fist and pounded the front of his head, the pain made it hard to think.

He dropped his hand and a sudden memory put a smile on his face. Jimmy could be of use after all. After he told Jimmy what he knew, Jimmy would do anything to keep him quiet.

*

Keeva watched Henry's face as they pulled up to the Senior Living Apartments. His mouth dropped open when they got out of the car.

"Wow. This is some nice place Mizz Betty lives in. This is a place for ladies like her." Looking from one end to the other of the sprawling white buildings, he pointed to the drive up portico. "It looks like a fancy hotel." His grin spread across his face.

"Yes, it is nice. Wait until you see the inside." Keeva smiled at Henry, touching his arm lightly to lead him to the building.

Betty greeted them at the entrance, kissing Keeva's cheek and giving Henry a bear hug. Henry blushed.

Betty led them through the large sitting area toward a receptionist who sat tapping a pen, signaling her impatience. As they approached, Betty leaned toward Keeva without taking her eyes off the receptionist, "This one is new, we call her Brunhilda." Keeva and Henry both covered their mouths, stifling laughter.

When they arrived in the apartment, Betty took their coats and motioned them to the living room area. Henry still looked like a man meeting royalty, eyes wide, head turning as he looked around the room with his mouth gaping. "Henry, why don't you help me in the kitchen? We can catch up and you can tell me how you've been," Betty said. They disappeared into the kitchen.

Keeva walked to the window that faced out to the parking lot. She enjoyed the view of the bright blue sky, and for the first time since the attack, she felt relaxed. Her request to meet at Betty's had been as much for her as Henry. The bright sunny apartment and Betty's loving support always smoothed out her worries.

Tony pulled into the parking lot and parked. She watched as he unfolded his large frame from his car and with one hand, threw a sports jacket over his shoulder. Just seeing his muscular physique sent feathery tingles through her stomach. He was dressed similar to the other morning, button-down shirt, tie and khaki pants, but from this distance without him noticing she could observe the whole package. And what a package it was. Betty and Henry moved into the room carrying enough food for the entire building.

She heard Betty telling Henry, "Well, Keeva's handsome boyfriend will probably ask the same questions, so I'll wait until he arrives to find out what this is all about. I don't want to make you have to answer twice."

Tony wasn't her boyfriend, but she knew contradicting Betty would confuse Henry. After all, she had been the one who had exaggerated when she'd told Henry that Tony was a good friend. Henry might not trust her or Tony, so she kept quiet. "Who told you he was good-looking?" she asked hoping Henry didn't repeat any of this conversation to Tony.

"You did, when you called me. I may be old, young lady, but I'm not senile. Do the words, dark and good-looking sound familiar?"

"You asked me what he looked like." Heat crept up her cheeks when she heard the knock at the door.

"Well, Detective Salazar," Betty said opening the door and holding out her hand. "What a pleasure it is to meet a friend of Keeva's."

"I don't think she'd call us friends, I'm probably more of a nemesis to her right now." Tony grinned, his large smile brightened his umber coloring.

Keeva stepped to the foyer and extended her hand. "It's good to see you again, Tony." His hand, large and rough, grasped hers gently.

After the greeting he turned to Henry, "You must

be Keeva's friend, I'm Detective Salazar," Tony held out his hand.

Keeva watched Henry closely, fearing he would freeze up, or worse yet, repeat the earlier conversation about Tony being her boyfriend. She held her breath but relaxed when Henry took the hand Tony had offered. His eyes refocused on the floor, and his shoulders remained hunched, a signal that they were still on tenuous ground on how Henry would handle the interview.

Keeva hoped he hadn't forgotten what he'd told her. She had been unable to find him and tracked down his landlord to get a message to him. It had been fortunate both Betty and Tony were available today. When they were seated in Betty's small but comfortable living room, Keeva spoke. "Remember, you said you saw someone outside the café. I know you already told me, but if you could tell Detective Salazar, he needs to hear it in your words."

"What do you want to know, Detective? I only saw him a little bit." Henry's soft voice was difficult to hear across the small room. He set his coffee on the table and pressed his hands together, between his knees. His eyes darted from person to person, then settled on Betty.

Watching Henry, Keeva knew she'd made the right decision. If the police had insisted on taking Henry to the police station, he would never have felt comfortable enough to talk. He felt safe with her and Betty. Betty gave Henry a reassuring smile, and his shoulders relaxed.

Keeva watched Tony lean his large frame forward, laying his forearms on his thighs, and folded his hands together, all his attention focused on Henry. He had put on the jacket before arriving at the apartment. She gazed at his bulging muscles pulling on his navy jacket. Something about his intense sexiness sent a tingle skittering up her neck.

"Let's start with the kids. Keeva said you told her you saw a man outside the café after the attack. Is that the only time you've seen him?" The gentleness in his voice surprised Keeva.

"No, no," he shook his head, "that man followed them a couple of times. The same man, each time I saw him. I don't remember how long ago when I saw him for the first time."

Tony looked at Keeva and lifted an eyebrow. She shrugged. Henry had not told her he saw them being followed before. He refocused on Henry and nodded. "Go on, Henry, tell me about all the times you saw him."

Henry's head bounced up and down like a bobble head doll. "Like I said, it always happened at night, and I couldn't see nothing but a man, a dark Unabomber shirt with the hood up. The Unabomber wore sunglasses, though."

"Unabomber shirt? I'm not sure I know what a Unabomber shirt is?"

"I think he means a hoodie," Keeva answered. "Henry told me about the hood being pulled up." She looked at Tony, "Remember, in the late nineties they flashed a sketch of the man they called the Unabomber. The hooded sweatshirt became synonymous with the Unabomber."

"I remember the photo, dark gray hoodie, dark sunglasses." Tony wrote something in his notebook. "Did you see where the kids went?"

"No. I can't move fast these days. Have a bum leg since I was a young'n. Just saw them going down the street and this man walking behind them, hiding in the trees and like." Henry's voice stayed at just above a whisper.

Henry continued. "I saw them go down Helena Avenue, but first them kids came out the alley, he came out behind them. But I didn't see them that night they got hurt." Henry chewed on a fingernail, his eyes darting back and forth. His eyes widened and Keeva knew he had just remembered something. "But I did see him a few nights ago, outside the cafe, when it was dark. I tol' Mizz Keeva 'bout that night. I go there because Mizz Keeva gives me the day-old bread and pastries." He blushed. "It isn't really day-old, she likes to pretend but I don't say anything. She is always nice to me."

He blushed and Keeva gave a small laugh, lifting her head and her eyes. Note to self, don't insult anyone's dignity with lies.

Tony looked sideways at Keeva, giving her a smile, not teasing like earlier. His eyes contained a softness. The smile relaxed the hard lines of his face and made him look easy-going and sweet. She took in a quick breath and turned away. She could not let herself think about him like that. He was not the soft kind.

Tony shifted, "When you see him, and it's dark, is it late at night or early in the morning?"

"It mostly be late at night. Too late for kids to be outside, but I suspect them kids don't listen anyhow. "Cept the other day when I came for the bread, then he was only in front of Mizz Keeva's, not following anyone." Henry nodded, very sure with his statement.

Stopping to take a break, Tony looked over the notes he had taken. Henry's story validated what Mac had told him and what Madison had confirmed. Madison had been adamant they'd been followed. According to her, on more than one occasion, she had seen someone standing in the shadows on side streets. Todd had told her he had never seen anyone.

Tony flipped the pages and found where he'd written down the conversation he'd had with Madison that morning when she had calmed down enough to talk to him about the attack. He remembered the conversation.

"We were walking through the alley, and Todd was teasing me because I was nervous." Someone committed a brutal attack against her. Her low hesitant voice and pale skin testified to the trauma. *"I didn't see anyone or anything strange, but Todd must have seen something. He put his arm around me and began moving us away from the wall of the alley. I looked up at him, he looked afraid."* She'd smiled a sad smile. *"Todd is never afraid of anything, but I wish he had been."*

Her mother had moved closer to Madison, and Tony had been afraid she'd stop the whole interview but Madison continued, *"We were almost running and I asked Todd what was wrong."* She'd wiped tears from her eyes with the back of her hand. *"Then I heard him behind us. I'm...I'm not sure, but I think he called Todd's name. I couldn't turn around because Todd had pulled me so tight and we were moving so fast. He said Todd's name. That's all he said, and then he, he.... She had begun sobbing and leaned into her mother's arms.*

Tony knew Madison would pay for the bastard's attack for a long time and he hadn't wanted to cause any further trauma. Putting off the questioning had annoyed him, but her hysteria had left him no choice.

Keeva stood to help Betty refill the drinks, and Tony felt the sudden coolness in the space next to him. He had been too aware of her sitting so near, and it had taken all his concentration to stay focused on Henry.

Distractions were rare for him, but being around Keeva forced him to focus on Henry because his mind kept drifting back to the striking woman next to him. Tony looked down at his notes, a poor attempt to refocus.

Betty and Keeva came back into the room with a tray of drinks and placed the silver tray on the coffee table. "How are those two young people, Detective?" Betty asked.

"Madison is fine. She didn't get hurt, physically." Tony remembered her pallor and felt anger at the perpetrator who caused so much suffering. "The last I heard the doctors were keeping Todd in an induced coma. His parents said they were going to begin waking him up for short periods of time soon." The doctors were cautiously optimistic Todd would recover, but they couldn't predict what lasting effects the trauma might cause.

"Oh, that poor child. I've been saying rosaries for him. I hope he gets well quickly," Betty crossed herself as she spoke. She paused and added, "And I hope they catch the bastard that did this." Her language surprised Tony, though apparently not as much as it surprised Henry. Henry's eyes lit up like headlights. Keeva looked unfazed. It was obvious she was used to the elegant woman cursing on occasion.

The dark mood that had haunted Tony the night of the attack fell over him again as he thought about Todd and the long road ahead of him. "Me too. And the sooner we catch the...." Tony almost slipped with *hijo de puta*, but held back. Calling him a son of a bitch wouldn't be professional. "The sooner we catch the culprit, the quicker we can lock him up."

Tony's cell phone vibrated in his pocket, but he ignored it, not wanting to interrupt Henry. He'd taken a liking to the older man. Henry spoke very simply, but had an impressive memory and understanding of the world around him.

"You're doing a good job, Henry. What you've told me so far has been very helpful. Do you think you can answer a few more questions? We're almost finished." He waited for Henry to acknowledge him. Tony wanted to keep the pace slow enough for Henry to remain comfortable.

"That's fine, Mr. Tony. You aren't scary like some policemen." Henry smiled.

"Thank you for the compliment, Henry, and I appreciate your cooperation."

"I want to help those kids."

"Good. So let me tell you what the girl told me and maybe that'll help you remember something else. Madison told me the man who hurt Todd knew his name. Did you ever see the man talking to them?"

Henry scratched his head. "Maybe. But just the

boy." Then he closed his eyes and scrunched his face as though thinking. "They talked, but not like friends. It was before the kids were hurt. Maybe last week."

Excitement ran though Tony. Maybe Henry had seen more than he realized. Tony put his hand up, he didn't want to interrupt Henry but he needed to pinpoint the location. "You saw this *same* man follow them down Helena Avenue?"

"Yes, the same man. But the kids turned on the next street just like the other nights."

Tony knew Madison lived one block over and she had said Todd always walked her to the door. "And when did he talk to Todd?"

"When the boy came by the alley, he was jogging like he did after taking the girl home. The man followed behind him." He stopped talking, furrowing his brow. "He was always hiding in the dark."

Tony smiled. Henry didn't see the irony. He had seen the man because Henry too had been hiding in the dark.

"The man, he stopped that boy. He called him, I heard it. He said *Todd* real loud." Henry relaxed back in his chair. "Yep. He knew his name."

"What did Todd do?" Tony asked.

"He stopped. I saw him turn to look at the man. The man went up to him."

Tony waited for more, but Henry just sat there. He needed more prodding. "What happened next,

Henry? Did the boy say something?" Tony leaned forward. The small love seat kept him and Keeva close, and he continued to find it difficult to concentrate on Henry with Keeva so near him. She radiated warmth, and something else, a perfume. A sweet and intoxicating perfume.

"They didn't talk nice. The words were loud. Then Todd said the bad F-word and ran away from the man." He shook his head and added, "I don't blame him. I wanted to say that word to the man, too."

Everyone laughed.

Tony began to get an eerie feeling about Keeva's involvement in this situation. Jimmy had left him a copy of the report he'd written up. In a later conversation they had concurred, Keeva probably had seen someone step out of the bushes the night she'd run home. He had a bad feeling. He was afraid she was his next target. When she had become a witness, she had put herself at risk, and now he didn't doubt the note had been a warning.

Tony had spoken with a profiler to get a better feel for what type of nut job they were dealing with. When she had seen the note, she had expressed concern over the wacko becoming fixated with Keeva. The bad feeling in Tony's gut supported that conclusion.

"Henry, I don't have any more questions. But with this man out there, I need you to do me a favor." He paused until Henry nodded. "Can you be careful, maybe not walk around at night?" Henry could be in as much danger as Keeva and he needed the man's reassurance he understood the importance of the request. "It's important you stay safe. if you've seen this man several times, he has probably seen you, too. You and Keeva have to be careful since he seems to lurk around the café at night. Can you promise me not to go to the café until morning?"

"Yes, Mr. Tony, I promise."

"Good, Henry."

"Yes, Henry. You're welcome to coffee and bread any time you'd like, but only in the daytime. To be safe," Keeva said.

Henry's face showed relief. "Thank you, Mizz Keeva."

Before they left the apartment, Tony pulled Keeva aside and told her he needed to talk to her away from Henry. She told him she had already spent too much time away from the café, but said to text her and they'd work out a time. He didn't like the delay. He worried she wasn't taking this as seriously as she ought to be, but he also didn't want to create panic.

Tony went back to the station, and a note from Scott, his supervisor, told him to call him when he returned from the interview with Henry. They had heard from Todd's parents. He was waking up, but slowly and for short periods. The doctors were optimistic about what they were seeing, but he was having some retrograde amnesia. Though happy Todd's prognosis looked good, he knew from experience that some people never regained memories of some past events, especially the trauma itself. If they did gain it back, in many cases it came back slowly, and in pieces. His hope for a quick resolution to the case began to dissolve.

Later that day, he sent Keeva a text: *Todd waking up, but not remembering. Need to ask you more questions. 6:30 tonite?*

Keeva responded: *Going 4 run w. Mac. Wrkng*

Then tomorrow. No excuse. Tony answered.

Wrkng late.

He wondered if it was an excuse. Excuses be damned, he wanted to see her.

I'll bring dinner. Time? Café?

K. 7:30. Yea. Tony almost felt the sigh in her response.

It's a date.

No d8. Wrkng dnnr.

Tony smiled.

CHAPTER 5

TONY FELL BACK into the door, scooping up his three-year old son who ran full force into his arms. His squeal of delight sent ripples of warmth through Tony. The stress and failure to find the perp was pushed aside, if only for a short time.

"Grrrhhhhh," he nuzzled his face into the tot's neck. "I'm the monster and I'm going to eat you up." TJ scurried off yelling more squeals of delight. Following the noise into the bedroom, he pulled back short as Mari emerged from the bathroom carrying a handful of toddler clothing and a green dinosaur towel.

"Mari," he said in an exaggerated loud voice, "have you seen a noisy child around here? I'm going to eat him for dinner."

"*Hermano*," she stood on her toes to kiss her brother on his cheek, "No, you will have to find him yourself."

Entering the bedroom, Tony pulled back the bed-covers earning laughs and giggles from his son. "Here, Papi, read this," the tyke pushed his favorite children's book into Tony's face.

Tony lay next to his son, smelling the fresh scent of soap, and read the book. Finishing the book, he looked over to see TJ asleep. He felt a tightening in his chest, as he thought about the long hours he had put in the last few days. Placing the book on the night-stand, he reached over, and pulled the bright-colored dinosaur quilt up to TJ's chin and pushed the black curls from the toddler's face. "Night, TJ, stay safe and have sweet dreams." He knew his son was asleep, but said the words anyway.

Before he had a son, he could never understand why people interrupted their lives and careers for them. Even leaving the stress of the CIA for a simpler life never had children in the plan. He figured they just became another form of anxiety. Nothing could be further from the truth. His son added more happiness to his life than he felt he deserved.

Standing at the door, Tony spent the next few minutes watching TJ sleep. Guilt tugged at him. Being a single parent who worked odd hours, he tried to put his son first but when a case came up he often had to work long hours. Since TJ's mom walked out of their lives and until Mari moved in several months ago, he had relied on daycare and babysitters.

Susie, TJ's mother, and Tony dated a short time. Wild and impulsive, she ended the relationship with an announcement she had found her soul mate in someone else. In the argument that followed, she accused him of being somber and secretive. He found no defense to counter her criticisms. Years living surreptitiously had left him suspicious of the world around him.

A battering ram to the face would have been mild compared to his surprise when Susie showed up at his door pregnant, declaring the baby was his and demanding they marry. A paternity test confirmed her allegation.

He understood his friends' concerns that she only wanted financial benefits but a proclivity to be honorable forced him to accept her proposal. They married within weeks and the troubled marriage lasted until TJ was eighteen months. For the second time, Tony had to endure her condescension as she walked out of his life. The divorce left him bitter and financially broke.

Looking at his son's sweet face and allowing the heart-stopping tenderness that surged in him always softened the resentment he harbored. He lived for TJ and knew that was all he needed in this world. So this new craving to include Keeva in his life perplexed him.

Could he take a chance again? The women he had dated always left him with the same chant, accusing him of being secretive and brooding. They had used different words, but the content had meant the same. But he'd never met one so caring as Keeva. A small glimmer sparked a tiny ray of hope. Maybe there could be someone who could understand him. He dropped his hand from the door frame and walked into the living room where Mari waited.

He inhaled as he walked into the living room, "What smells so good?"

"*Ropa vieja. Tienes hambre?*" His sister's offer of food tempted him, though the literal English translation, *old clothes*, did little to convey the savory flavor of the Cuban national dish.

"I have plans, but save me some leftovers and I'll take them for lunch. Did you already eat?"

"I'll eat later. I have some work to do."

"You're as thin as a rail. As soon as this case is over, I'm taking a few days off and I'm going to fatten you up."

"Listen to you, you sound like *Mami*." She put her laptop on the coffee table. "It's bad enough having a macho cop brother. Don't add to it by worrying about my eating habits."

Tony bit the inside of his mouth and swallowed down a groan. Mari had always been brilliant and it would become both a blessing and a curse for her.

After graduating high school early, she had gone to an accelerated advanced degree program at college. Being much younger had left her isolated and less mature than her peers. Her innocence left her vulnerable to an older man who had taken advantage of her naiveté and he used her financial brilliance to further his illegal dealings. The company folded when several high-level employees had been charged with racketeering, including Mari.

If it had not been for Tony's connections in the government, she could have gone to prison. Tony had pulled every favor owed to him to have the federal government dig deeper until they had found her boyfriend had framed her. Between the betrayal and the media's despairing write-ups, she had sunk into a depression.

She had lost weight and had become a recluse. Her parents and Tony had hoped that leaving Miami for a new scene and being around TJ would begin to give her purpose again. Mari had agreed, and her rise from her gloom became evident in a few short weeks after moving to Montana and caring for TJ. It had also benefitted TJ.

Before Mari arrived, TJ had begun to ask more frequently about his mother. The most honest thing Tony could tell TJ was that his mother had to work and it kept her away. It had been only half-true. Susie's idea of working was finding the next boyfriend who could support her.

Tony didn't even know where Susie lived. He would contact her sister and leave a message and Susie would call him back on her sister's phone. They both knew the marriage had been a mistake, but Tony never understood how she had seen TJ as a mistake, too.

TJ had begun asking less about his mother and seemed to be happier. Tony knew it couldn't last. As Mari moved past the hurt, she had begun to talk about traveling. Just last week she told him she had begun planning an extended trip to Spain. Tony was happy his sister was moving on, but he still hated what she had gone through.

He was such an ass. The direct approach worked at work, but he would forget to turn off the bullish behavior at home. Mari needed to learn to find her own way, and he had to be careful not to smother her.

After a shower and spending a little too much time on his hair, he stood facing the clothes he laid on the bed. He picked up a bright, navy long-sleeve shirt, held it next to his chest looking in the mirror and threw it down. He wanted to make a good impression, not look like a pimp. Pulling out a white button-down, it looked like he was still working, but at least she wouldn't think he was trying to jump in her pants. He grabbed a tie and started to tie it, but a glimpse in the mirror told him she'd think he was on official business. He dumped the tie, opened the top two buttons, and put on a black leather jacket. He walked out of the room, knowing he would never leave the house if he kept this up. It didn't stop the jitters in his stomach.

"Wow," Mari eyed him up and down. "Where are you going looking all *sexy*?" She grinned up at Tony as he walked down the stairs. He had known she would be curious, as he rarely made plans on a weeknight. "It must be someone special?"

He tugged the lapels of the fitted leather jacket. "It's nothing serious. She's just part of an investigation." He felt like a liar even as he said the words. He'd always been the love them and leave them type, but something about Keeva made him feel different. Every time he saw her, he wanted to erase the space between them and every time he left her, he wanted the time until he'd see her again to disappear.

Grabbing the bag he had packed up in the kitchen he stepped back into the living room. Mari, who still worked with intense concentration on her computer, smiled at him.

"I'll see you later," he said as he leaned down and kissed her on her head.

*

Tony could see a lone car in the parking lot. He hoped it was hers and that she had driven to work this morning instead of jogging. A cloak of darkness blanketed the front of the café, while the back kitchen was ablaze in glowing lights. He knocked at the rear door, the only one with the light on. "It's open," he heard her yell. He couldn't believe she had left the door unlocked. Anyone could have walked in. With a flat palm he smacked at the door, pulling his hand back before it connected.

Pushing the door open, he could see her standing over a stove, stirring. She looked at him, smiled and his anger softened. He piled the bags on the counter as she went back to what she stirred on the stove. Standing still, he watched her. She was tall and athletic looking. She wasn't skinny like so many women he usually dated, but muscular and strong. He wondered if she would feel as solid as she looked or whether she'd feel softer than she appeared.

"What are you making?"

"Sauces I use for the fillings." She frowned. "It's why I had to work late the last few nights. On top of everything else, we think someone threw a few batches out."

Irritation at the person who would cause more work for Keeva burned in his chest. He placed his hands, a little too hard, down on the counter. "On top of everything else? What else is going on?" He didn't understand the baking business, but if something was wrong, his money was on Tighe being the culprit.

Her eyes closed, Keeva took in a long deep breath.

"It's all of it. Someone breaking in, supplies missing, expensive supplies arriving that we didn't order. Now the sauces." She hesitated. She stopped stirring as if lost in thought, and then she jumped and began an exaggerated stirring. "I make them and freeze them, and they are used for the fillings of the pastries. It's my grandmother's recipes. Nobody but Mac has access to the recipes."

"And why would someone throw out your sauces?" He began removing the food he had brought from the bags.

"I don't know. I stock a freezer in the basement, and it all disappeared." She paused like she wanted to say something, but stopped.

Tony wondered what she had been thinking. "So I'm making more, but just enough for a few nights at a time. It's expensive, milk, cream, eggs, vanilla beans. I only use fresh ingredients. Heck, I need a small loan for the vanilla beans alone. I have them shipped in from Tahiti." The spoon rattled in the pot as she stirred more aggressively. Picking up a small spoon, she dipped it in the sauce and he watched as the creamy yellow sauce dripped off. She wiped a finger slowly over the spoon, placing the contents that dripped down her finger into her mouth. Her lips and their movement mesmerized him.

An X-rated movie didn't have near the seductive power she did with that one act. She removed her fingers, furrowed her forehead, and confusion registered on her face. He realized he had been staring and cleared his throat, "Um, do you think someone took it and didn't throw it out?" He had been checking up on Tighe and had found out he had been released from Deer Lodge Prison six months ago. He wondered if Keeva knew that. But why would an ex-con steal vanilla sauce?

She turned off the stove, moved the pot and turned to him. "What good would it do them? It was a hell of a lot of sauce. Besides, I can't imagine any of my employees doing that." She washed her hands in the sink. "I think I mislabeled the date and someone threw them out. The health department is sticky about that."

She started rummaging through the food he brought. "It all looks good, but it's quite a bit for two of us."

Tony felt like a world-class idiot. "I didn't know what you liked, so I brought a little of everything." He pulled out some containers, "Thai curried chicken and in case you don't eat meat, this one is vegetarian." He pointed to the last bag, "These are salads, in case you want a salad."

She angled her head at him, her green eyes looked bright under the industrial lights. "You are a funny man, Tony. I took you for a take it or leave it guy, and here you are concerned about what I'd eat." Her lips turned up in a grin.

Tony, shuffled his feet, he couldn't believe he was so nervous. It was just a working dinner. But he wanted it perfect. "I guess I could have called." She grinned at him, and unlike him, she looked relaxed.

"It's fine. I'm a burger girl myself. But since there's Thai food and I hardly ever buy it, I'll take that." She began reaching for plates. "I have wine and beer, or are you on duty, as they say?"

"Beer's fine. I'm technically off, someone else is on call."

In the dining room, they split the Thai food, taking a little of each.

Keeva thought of asking him why he was there if he was off duty, but knew any answer would be the wrong one. Like a seesaw, her feelings about tonight had vacillated. A conundrum rose within her, she wanted to see him, though each time she saw him, she liked him more. If seeing him meant having feelings for him, she'd rather not see him.

After a few minutes of silent eating, Tony asked, "How much do you know about Tighe?"

"My baker?"

"Is there another Tighe that works here?"

"Just him. He came here about six months ago. He worked for several bakeries in the past, plus he'd trained as a pastry chef." She wondered what Tighe had to do with anything.

"Where was he trained, Sing Sing School of Chefs?" His voice sounded as sarcastic as his words.

Keeva was surprised at his sharp words and sat back staring at him.

He studied her silently for a moment, then with a twitch that passed for a smile said, "I'm sorry, I didn't mean to be so harsh."

She was confused, what would Tighe have to do with all of this?

Tony took a sip of the beer. "Do you know he spent six months in Deer Lodge Prison?" His voice was much softer.

"Yes, he told me." It sounded weak, and she knew if Mac or Betty knew about his record and that she'd still hired him, they would be furious. "He said he'd made some bad choices, trusted a few people who turned out to be unsavory. He got into some tax issues, I believe."

"And you still hired him?"

Keeva put her fork down. "Have you ever tried to find a baker in a small city, and one who will work nights for as little as I can pay? I did background and reference checks." Hiring an ex-con had bothered Keeva, but she hadn't had any choice. When she'd hired him, he'd sounded contrite, so she'd given him a chance to start over. But over time he had begun to abuse her generosity. She knew he had been lax about his hours, but right now she had few options.

"Point accepted. As long as you know who you have working for you." They ate in silence for a while.

She wanted him to know how hard it had been for her to hire Tighe. "I tried for six months." Her words were soft.

"Tried what?"

Why she wanted to explain what she couldn't say, but she needed Tony to understand her limited choices. "I had been doing all the baking. The recipes were Nana's, my grandmother's, and at first I thought I could do it all. I didn't want anyone else to have them." She remembered the excitement and joy when she had first opened. "But after a year, we had become so busy, I had to put more time in during the day. The work became too much. I couldn't work days and nights." She started piling their empty plates.

Tony put his hand on hers, stilling her movements. "You don't need to explain. I just saw his prison tattoos and checked into it."

His firm hand, warm and reassuring, offered a comfort she hadn't felt in a long time and until now, hadn't realized she'd missed it.

They cleared the table, and Keeva began washing dishes in the large metal industrial sink. Tony carried the last few dishes and placed them in the sink. His muscular arms brushed against hers. She moved to give him room, and his large frame moved into the space she had vacated. Trying to ignore her awareness of him, she put her energy into finishing the dishes as he put the food away.

After filling plastic containers with the two sauces she had made, she picked some up to carry down stairs. "I'll just take these down and I'll be ready to lock up."

He walked over to her. "Here, let me take some of them." He scooped them from her arms.

"Is this the dungeon where you keep all the bodies?" His chuckle sounded loud as they entered the cavernous basement.

They both spied the splintered door at the same time. Freezing in front of it, the air in the room became too thick to breathe. "I don't get it. All of the other problems." A weariness permeated her and she wanted it all to go away. "Now this." She gestured to the splintered door.

"What the hell?" He swiveled, looking for somewhere to place the containers, setting them on a nearby table. Tony examined the door. "It looks like they took a crowbar, or something similar to it. I'm guessing those pins are so old they are frozen in and whoever did this couldn't get it open." He peeled a piece of the splintered wood close to one of the hinges.

Keeva, unable to take a deep breath, felt her legs tremble and dropped onto an empty overturned five-gallon ice cream tub. The cold concrete cooled her back as she sagged against the old cement wall.

He put a hand out to help her up. She wanted to stay there, to have all the problems go away, but she took his hand and let him pull her up. He held onto her hand after she was upright. His large hand, strong and supportive, held on to her firmly. She wanted to accept the support it offered, but that was a fantasy. He was simply doing his job. She tugged her shaking hand back. "The night of the attack, I think someone was trying to get into the basement. The baking rack was right in front of the door, but with the lights out, they didn't see it and knocked it over," she said in a low voice, acknowledging as much to herself as Tony.

After putting away the sauces, Keeva locked the door and Tony double-checked it. She walked to the basement stairs, waiting for Tony to go ahead of her. She kept talking as they ascended the stairs.

"Lucy tells me we had some supplies missing, not a lot, but enough for her to notice. A week later, a huge order came in, all stuff neither one of us ordered." She locked the basement door after they stepped back into the kitchen. "Since then two more have come in, all the invoices show our name and address as placing the order. Only we didn't place those them." She sat on a stool and faced Tony. "Lucy signed for them thinking I ordered them."

He crossed his arms watching her, "Would there be a reason for her not to question the orders?"

"She did after the second order. It's common for one of us to place an order and tell the other about it later. But three pretty big orders without me telling her surprised her so she asked me about it." Keeva nervously scratched one of her palms. The orders, the missing supplies, it had all seemed preposterous, but now, saying the words aloud gave them conviction.

Tony pulled up another stool, moving it in front of her as he sat. His knees brushed against hers, sending a rush of heat through her. She had flipped off all but a small light by the door. The darkened room caused his skin to look a deeper bronze against his white shirt. Men were not supposed to look so perfect.

"Then the sauce issue," he finished her list of mysteries. "Do you think you have a competitor sabotaging you?"

"I don't know. That's what Lucy thinks, but it baffles me." She rubbed her forehead.

"It'll be fine. I'll send someone over in the morning to take a report." He grabbed her other hand. "Crap, you're freezing. You need to get home, crawl under the covers and get a good night's sleep."

She didn't want him to let go of her hand, and he didn't. He kept rubbing it. "I spoke with Jimmy Smith, and he told me about the other night."

She wanted to flee at the embarrassing memory.

She swallowed. "Oh, God," she rolled her head to the side and pulled her hand away. How humiliating. "It was nothing, I was just spooked."

"No, I don't believe that and neither does Jimmy." His hands landed on her knees. A part of her wished he wouldn't keep touching her. But why did it feel so good if she didn't want him to?

"Listen Keeva, I'm not trying to embarrass you. There is some asshole out there and he deserves all the blame. I just want you to be careful." He squeezed her knees.

Keeva enjoyed his strong touch, but knew it was a dangerous sensation. Her life would be simpler without complications. No matter what she wished, each time his warm hands connected with her sensitive skin it stirred something deep inside her. He squeezed again. "Promise me you'll be careful?" She moved his hands away. His deep luscious brown eyes scanned her face in anticipation.

He wasn't finished, "No more running alone and no more," he pointed to the kitchen door, "unlocked doors?"

Thankfully, he let go of her. "I promise. I'll drive everywhere." She had used a good chunk of her dwindling savings to pay for car insurance, but unless gas was free, she'd have no choice but to ride her bike on occasion.

Since she had driven to the café that morning, she

drove home. Tony followed her in his car and walked her to the door. Her apartment, part of a house built in the 1890s, had originally been built to be quarters for live-in help. A side entrance opened to a small foyer. To the left, a locked door led to the main house. Straight ahead, a set of stairs led to her apartment. After she had unlocked the first door to the outside, Tony held her back with his hand. He walked in ahead of her. "Is this to the main house?"

She nodded. He checked the knob and the door didn't budge. He went up the stairs, his hand moving her behind him. When they reached the top he leaned back while she unlocked the door to her apartment. She had begun to push the door open as Tony put his hand over her mid-section. "Let me check it out." She watched as he pulled out a Glock from inside his jacket, and made his way into her apartment. Keeva sighed. All she wanted to do was go to sleep.

He stepped into the apartment, sweeping the room with his gun. When he walked into the bedroom, bursts of heat fanned her face knowing her bed was a mess. She watched as he moved through the room, checked the closet and even under the bed. She hoped the dust bunnies stayed hidden.

She followed behind him, keeping some distance in case he mistook her for an intruder.

"All clear?" She asked teasing as they came out of the bedroom. He glared at her, and she stifled a giggle.

"It's not funny."

"I'm sorry. I do take it seriously. But if I don't laugh Tony, the alternative is not a pretty sight."

"Lock behind me."

After he left, Keeva flopped onto the couch. She should be afraid, she should be angry, she should be something other than confused.

Her emotions gripped her and vacillated between fear and concern all the way to comfortable. It had been a long time since she had felt comfortable about anything. The finances kept her stressed like an over-tightened violin string. Yet Tony's reassurance had relaxed her. The past week had been a roller coaster of emotions, frightening events, and alarming mysteries. Spending the evening with Tony had lessened her stresses. Even the damaged closet seemed a trifle event with his reassurance.

But reality set in. What would he see in her? He'd always dressed so sharp, while her idea of dressing up was a new pair of hiking boots. The most she styled her hair was to pull it back and try and tame the curls. Besides, she had an independent backbone scared most men she dated. Why would he be any different?

He wanted to solve the case and mark another notch in his belt. He had brought dinner, he was kind, but maybe he was kind to all the women he knew. She could fill a tea cup with all she knew about him. She suspected he kept it that way.

She didn't want to move from the couch, but she needed a hot shower. She still felt cold. The weather in Montana could be capricious in March, snowy one minute, warm the next. The past week had been as cold as the mood had been dreary.

After raising the thermostat, she took a hot shower. Warm and wrapped in her fleece pink robe, the concerns she had earlier had washed away with the hot water. Deciding she deserved a small treat, she pulled open the drawer for her favorite silk pajamas. Reaching for them, she spotted a small piece of paper sitting on top. Her hand froze. Little stick figures, tormenting and evil, stared back at her.

She stumbled to her bed, grabbing her purse. Her fingers shook so hard she had little control over them. She willed them to work. Somehow, she got them to press the 9-1-1 before her world went black.

*

It looked like a macabre block party when Tony arrived at Keeva's apartment. The lights from the police cars and an ambulance whirled colors through the night. They created an eerie carnival atmosphere. Curious neighbors had piled out of their homes, concerned over whatever had disturbed their peace. Several police officers standing by the walkway to the apartment nodded at Tony when he passed them.

Inside the apartment, the atmosphere was also alarming, but without the eerie lights. He almost bumped into Gary, who was talking to Lizbeth, a female patrol officer. "We've got to stop meeting like this." Gary's humor missed its mark and Tony ignored the comment.

"Where's Keeva?"

Gary's face registered confusion. "In there," he said tipping his head in the direction of Keeva's bedroom. "She's fine. She just fainted. She had regained consciousness by the time the police arrived. What's wrong with you?"

Before Tony could respond, Mac walked out of the bedroom and approached him. "What the hell is going on? She says this is the second note."

Tony shook his head. "I don't know. Let me talk to her and make some sense of this." Tony moved around Mac and walked into the bedroom. Keeva was sitting on the bed, wearing a bathrobe, with one of the ambulance blankets thrown over her shoulders. Her wet hair, tucked under the blanket, had created a dark irregular design. She visibly trembled. The paramedic's blood pressure cuff deflated and he stood.

"Your blood pressure's better but I think you should at least go to the ER."

Keeva looked up at him, "No, I'm fine." Her voice was shaky. A hollowness filled Tony's stomach, seeing her so vulnerable.

Lizbeth handed Tony a clear envelope. Inside Tony could see a yellow paper with two stick figures, exactly like the ones from the first note. The male and a female with a wild mane of hair had their arms extended as though holding hands. This time there were no words.

Tony knelt in front of Keeva and grabbed her hands. They felt like ice. She didn't look up at him so he lifted her chin. Her red-rimmed eyes searched his. "How did he get in here?" she asked in a soft, shaky voice.

He felt an ache in his chest hearing the pain in her voice. "I don't know. But I will find out and I'll make sure he never gets in here again. I promise." Tony wished he could kill the son of a bitch who kept haunting her.

Tony looked up at Lizbeth and returned the evidence bag to her. "What did they find?"

"It looks like there are a few scratches at both the lower and upper doors. So he probably picked the locks."

"Were you the first one here?" Tony asked.

She nodded. "We got the 9-1-1 call and dispatch said the caller didn't respond. She told me the name and address and I recognized the name. The shift reports said to keep an eye out in this area." Lizbeth blew out a breath and shook her head. "Keeva must have come to right before I got here, because I knocked on the door and she opened it." Lizbeth pinched her lips and looked like she had more to say, but held back. She pointed with her chin for Tony to move away from Keeva.

"Stay with her. I'll be right back." Tony said to the two paramedics as he stood. He wondered why one stood back against the wall not moving and the other one did all the work. Tony didn't recognize the medic by the wall, maybe he was new. He stepped into the living room with Lizbeth and pulled the bedroom door shut.

"What is it?" Tony leaned back against the wall. He would rather be in there with Keeva, but needed to find out as much as he could.

"I'm not sure. It's like the guy is invisible. I mean, half the department is driving around in this area, especially the café and this house." Lizbeth shifted uncomfortably. "I ate my dinner in the car across from her house earlier. Honest to God, I didn't see anyone."

Tony put a hand on Lizbeth's shoulder. "Don't worry. This is on the idiot doing all this, not on you or anyone else. I'll consider what you said and look at how someone could have access to our comings and goings."

Lizbeth didn't look any more relieved, she just shrugged, and walked away.

The paramedic who'd seemed to do all the work walked up to him as Tony walked back in the bedroom. He didn't see Keeva, but the bathroom door was closed and he guessed she had gone in there. "She doesn't want to go to the ER so we're done here. Her vitals are normal, but it would be best if she were cleared by a doctor."

The new medic, tall and skinny, slouched against the wall and lingered in the room. Most of the paramedics kept a neat, professional appearance but this guy's stringy brown hair needed a cut, and from the sheen, probably a wash. Tony saw him staring at the closed door of the bathroom. Was the young man freaked out by the recent attacks? Scary situations were all part of the job, and he'd better get over the nerves if he was going to be a paramedic and help people in urgent situations.

He didn't have time to think about this guy, he had to concentrate on Keeva and who continued to harass her.

Mac joined him. "Is she okay?"

"The paramedics say she's fine. She's in there," he pointed toward the bathroom door.

Mac glanced at the door, and then returned his focus to Tony. "How the hell did someone get in here?" Mac whispered.

"He picked the locks. I'm going to call a security company. The owner worked in the CIA with me. It might take him a few days to get here, so in the meantime you and I need to stay with her."

"What security are you talking about?" Keeva's sharp voice startled Tony.

"I have a friend who owns a high-tech security company out of L.A. I'm going to have him send someone out to put locks and cameras here and at the café." Tony said.

Keeva closed her eyes and shook her head. "No."

"No?" Both men spoke in unison.

"I can't afford it. I've seen systems on sale at Discount Mart and I can put in a deadbolt myself." She had changed into jeans and a sweater, but crossed her arms and rubbed them as though she was still cold. Tony saw the blanket on the bed and picked it up. He placed it over her shoulders, his arm crossing her back. He held it there for a second, not wanting to let go. He wanted to hold her and not let her out of his sight. "You don't have to worry about the cost. He owes me a favor."

"But if he charges, I'll pay for it," Mac added. "And if it's more than I can afford we can talk to Betty."

Keeva's eyes widened. "Don't you dare tell Betty about any of this." She sounded adamant.

"Okay, okay." Mac held up his hands, palms forward in defense. "We don't have to tell her anything."

"I'll take care of it. I can get one of the security systems I've seen on sale and do the deadbolt." Her voice took on a stubborn tone. She pulled the blanket tighter, and swayed.

Tony grabbed her, "Damn it," he huffed and led her to an overstuffed chair in the corner of the room, where he sat her down. "That isn't an option. I'll get new locks in the morning and call Chris. I don't want this asshole to get near you again."

Mac lifted an eyebrow. "You sure this Chris guy will come here?"

"Don't worry, he will." Tony had saved Chris's life when they had been tracking a cell of terrorists through Eastern Europe. Chris had said the debt hadn't been paid, that the trip to Montana to install Tony's security system had been as fun as a vacation. Tony figured two more systems would even the score.

"Can I get up, please?" Tony hadn't realized he was pressing down on Keeva's shoulder. "I'd like to make a cup of tea."

The three of them went into the living room, only to find that everyone had gone. Tony led Keeva to the couch. She kept pulling the blanket tighter. He couldn't figure if she was still cold, or if she was gaining a sense of false protection from the blanket.

"I might have to go to Denver in the next day or two," Tony said. "Todd is waking up and Chief Becker wants me to talk to him." Tony glanced at Keeva, her brows pulled together, in a questioning expression. He sat next to her and placed a reassuring hand on her leg. "I had hoped we could switch on and off here, but I need to get to the office tomorrow, and I'll probably have to leave right after that."

Mac nodded, "I can stay, but first I need to get

back to the apartment and lock it up. I also need to make arrangements with a neighbor I was supposed to drive to work tomorrow morning at around five."

Tony trusted Mac, but felt better if he were the one to stay tonight. He needed Mac fresh tomorrow when he had to leave. "Why don't I stay tonight? That way you can drive your neighbor and relieve me in the morning. When I get to the office, I'll send someone over to put in the deadbolts." Mac nodded in agreement "But before you head out, can you wait here a minute? I'll run to the car and get the overnight bag I keep there."

Tony realized he still held on to Keeva's leg and pulled his hand back. "It'll be two or three days before I'm back, will you be okay?"

"Not a problem." Mac gave a nod to Tony.

Tony retrieved his overnight bag while Keeva made tea. After Mac left, Tony propped a chair under the door knob, and placed a few pans on the chair seat. If someone did come in, they'd make a hell of a racket and then he'd mop the floor with the SOB's face.

"You know I hate that, or the idea of that." She pointed to his temporary security solution.

"What, you don't like my handiwork?" He pretended to pout.

"No." She sat at the table, her hands wrapped around a cup of tea that remained untouched. "I don't like the idea I have to put that in front of my door or that I have to have a babysitter."

"Oh, but I read the best bedtime stories. And I do a super job of tucking someone into bed." He liked the idea of putting her into bed and not necessarily to sleep.

"Tony, I have a thirty-eight revolver and I'm an excellent shot. You don't need to stay here. I'll just keep the gun next to me on the night stand." She sounded like she was pleading, but she kept stealing nervous glances at the front door.

He wanted to keep the mood light, but he needed to reassure her. "Are you saying you don't like my company?" He smiled, leaned forward and placed his hands over hers around the mug of tea. She stilled, her eyes watching his movements. He slid his hands under hers, and lifted them. Intertwining their fingers, he squeezed, just a bit, just enough to reassure her. With their hands twined in front of them, he said, "Keeva, unless you use that gun and shoot me, I'm not leaving here until Mac is here to replace me in the morning. I told you I'd keep you safe and I will."

Her green eyes began filling with tears, and he thought his heart would break. She sucked in a deep breath, pulling her arms back and wiping her tears with her palms. "Thank you, Tony." Her lips moved into a small smile. "Somehow you are there at all the right moments."

He didn't feel that way. If he had been there at the right times, he'd have caught the bastard when he broke in and they'd be picking him up in pieces. "Hey, who else would carry your jars of sauce for you?" He winked at her.

Keeva stood, "Yeah, where would I be if I had to do all that work myself."

She brought Tony some sheets and blankets from the closet and then she made a second trip and came out with three pillows.

"How many people are you expecting?" He teased as he took the pile of pillows from her.

"That couch is old and lumpy, so they'll come in handy," she said.

He placed them on the couch and spread out a sheet. "I've slept on a lot worse so I'm sure it'll be fine."

She smiled at him then turned and walked into her bedroom, shutting the door behind her.

About two in the morning, Tony sat up from the couch and turned on his smart phone. Pain pressed behind his eye and he knew a headache of gargantuan proportions waited for him. A night light offered enough illumination for him to make his way to the bathroom where he found ibuprofen tablets in the cabinet. In the hall, on his way back to the lumpy couch, the light in the hall went on and the brightness blinded him. The bright light pierced his eye, sending shards of pain into his already pounding head. He threw his hand up to cover his eyes.

"Sorry," Keeva said. She turned the light off, plunging them back into semi-darkness.

"It's okay." Tony rubbed the side and front of his head with his thumb and forefinger. The pain caused by the light lingered in a throb behind his eye.

"I couldn't sleep and heard you. Is everything okay?" She began walking to the kitchen and Tony followed.

"I feel a headache coming. I hope you don't mind I took some ibuprofen from the medicine cabinet."

"Help yourself to what you need." She opened the refrigerator, "I have water, juice, wine and beer? What's your poison?" She stood waiting for his answer.

"Water is fine." He smiled.

She handed him one, poured herself a glass of juice, and wandered back into the living room where she pulled a quilt from a nearby overstuffed chair and flopped onto it. She folded her long legs underneath her. "So what keeps you up at night?" She sipped her juice.

The dim light cast a light glow around her, softening her features. Her smooth skin and heart shaped face, accented by hair that was the color of wheat right before harvest. Curls, pointed in every direction, framed her face.

"Everything," he paused, reflecting before letting

the words come out. "I don't like it that this case is still open, and it bothers me I'm not doing my job." He wanted to tell her the worst of it all had been that he hadn't kept the nut job away from her but he held back. Reminding her of his failure could only make her feel worse.

"Well, here you are. And that is probably beyond any job requirement. I appreciate it." She leaned to the side, placing her glass on the table and pulled the bright-colored quilt up to cover her arms. "Why do you think he's bothering me?"

Bothering? That was the understatement of the year. "I suspect it has something to do with the attack. We know he had been in the area before the attack, Henry and Madison both support that, but he didn't have any focus on you prior to attacking Madison and Todd. At least not that we know of. My suspicion is you being a witness and saving them put his focus on you."

She hugged her knees. "That's a winner. Be a Good Samaritan and become a victim." Her voice trailed off as she dropped her head to her bent legs, resting it on her knees.

Tony leaned over to her and lifted her chin. Her green eyes searched his. The anger he read in her eyes surprised him. "I know this isn't easy. But Mac and I will keep you safe."

She squinted her eyes and balled her fists. Tony

wasn't surprised at her anger, he could imagine the frustration she must be feeling. He stiffened, prepared for the onslaught.

Keeva pulled back, threw the quilt back and stood. "I don't want you or anyone else's protection. I want to get my gun and shoot the son of a bitch. I want to have my life back and stop having people treat me like a helpless child." Her green eyes blazed, and she held her arms stiff at her side, fists still clenched tight.

Tony sat still, knowing she needed to vent.

Her voice escalated as she spoke. "How can one idiot control everything and a whole freaking police department can't even figure out who he is?"

Tony put his hands up in defense. "Hey, I'm sorry this guy was here, and I wish I'd done more." He'd much rather see her like this, angry, ready to take on the entire police department rather than frightened and helpless. She hadn't bothered pulling her hair back, and it flew out wildly like her indignation. Most women would whimper and hide, but not Keeva. She reminded him of a ferocious kitten, all spit and fire. He doubted she wanted a response so he held back allowing her to expel her frustration with the situation. He'd braced for another round of venting but she took several deep breaths, and appeared to gather her composure.

Tony opened his mouth to tell her he understood her anger, but before he could speak she cut him off.

"I hope your headache gets better." With that, she turned away and walked back to her room. Perhaps her outburst had given her a sense of control and that one of them might get some sleep.

Mac knocked at five. "I figured you'd have to get to work," Mac whispered when Tony opened the door.

"Thanks." Tony disliked the idea of leaving now. He wanted to let Keeva know he understood the frustration she'd expressed and that everything would be okay. He wanted to tell her he'd find this idiot. But he knew Todd might be the only person who could identify his attacker. Feeling he left things unsaid, he knew right now finding Todd's attacker was the best way he could help Keeva.

*

Keeva had sat on the edge of her bed until she heard Mac. She had struggled with the urge to go back and apologize to Tony for her explosion, but she had talked herself out of it. Her father had called her stubbornness and quick temper, Irish passion, but she doubted Tony would agree. He had looked at her with surprise as though he was seeing her for the first time. Now she felt like an idiot.

When she heard the door shut, she guessed Tony had bolted out of there before he would have to deal with her again. He had spent the night to protect her, and she had treated him as though he were the problem.

"Hey," Mac said when she walked into the kitchen. He was eating a bowl of cereal. Keeva wondered how anyone could eat now.

She poured a glass of milk from the container on the table.

"How are you this morning?" Mac asked.

"Just as you would figure, tired, angry and wanting this whole thing over." They sat in silence for several minutes.

"It will be, sis. There are enough cop cars in this area, as soon as the jerk shows his face, they'll get him." He placed a hand over hers.

"I want to believe you, but right now I don't feel reassured. I feel frustrated." With all her energy drained between the night's events and lack of sleep, she didn't even feel like having the conversation.

CHAPTER 6

SLUMPED IN THE old floral overstuffed chair in the work lounge, he glanced at his co-worker who prattled all morning to another employee. "Can you believe it? The guy broke into her apartment." The co-worker shoveled a fork full of food in his mouth and continued, "What a moron," the food garbling his words, "you know the police will get him now." He wanted the worker to choke so he'd stop talking. When that didn't happen, he distracted himself by focusing on last night's events. He managed to shut out the co-worker's rants the rest of the day.

After work he went home and packed a few things before leaving for the cabin. A stroke of genius on his part had been gaining the use of the cabin. He had the next two days off and planned to use them to prepare for Keeva. His half-brother rarely used the place, so he figured it was fair game. He often wondered why the moron didn't sell it, or better yet, just give it to him. It should have been his, along with the surrounding property.

He carried plywood boards into the building to cover up the windows. When he brought Keeva here he wanted the place to look as deserted as it had been lately. There weren't many people in the area, but even a small light could carry quite a distance in the remote area. Time, he just needed more time to convince her she belonged with him.

The cabin faced the road, but a stream ran behind it. The long dirt road that led to it rarely had visitors. He looked over at the stream. Nearby a circle of tree trunks lay on their sides. The tree trunks, vestiges of their glory days, had been the campfire seats when The Free Militia had gathered here. But now the earth worked at reclaiming them.

He walked over to the largest stump and righted it. He sat down in the spot where his father had sat on cool nights. The other members and their families had encircled a roaring fire and listened to his father's speeches. His father would bellow over the roaring blaze about the upcoming take over by the people who illegally ran the United States Government.

His father's predictions had come to fruition. Many of the members had lost their land and moved on, and the militia disbanded. Lars Smith, his father, had called it a conspiracy.

The cabin had belonged to Lars' first wife Jane. Lars and Jane were married a short time when she'd inherited a small fortune from her grandparents, which included the family's hunting cabin. Lars had seen it as a gift from God and proof he should build his militia. Lars then moved his young family to live full-time in the cabin. The isolation and rustic living overwhelmed Jane and she suffered bouts of depression. For months on end she'd become bed ridden, even unable to care for her son.

One day Lars came in from hunting and found her and their son gone. She'd taken their son and moved back to Capital City. When she tried to kick Lars out of the cabin and keep him from any contact with their son, he'd threatened to reveal Jane's depression and use it as a weapon to take the boy from her. In time she'd relented and agreed to allow Lars to live in the cabin and see their son during the summer. Soon they divorced.

Lars had eventually brought home a new wife. As Lars' second son, this cabin was the only home he'd ever known.

As far as he knew, Jane had never stepped foot on the property again. Though she'd kept her promise to let Lars remain in the cabin and grant visiting rights with their son.

The dark purpled nights and the scent of pine trees mixed with the cadence of his father's talks were the memories he kept in the forefront. At times, the memories of his father's beatings, his older half-brother abandoning them, squeezed his brain and the headaches would return.

Keeva will help them go away. He'll have her and then none of the bad will return.

He hadn't understood the legalities growing up, but he knew no other home. Lars said possession was nine-tenths of the law and that someday it would be his. Adverse possession, his father called it. He'd said because they let them live there they owned it.

Lars was a big man and never appeared sick, but one day he dropped dead. A heart attack. Two months later the sheriff showed up and said they had thirty days to vacate. He argued with the sheriff, repeating his father's words – adverse possession. The sheriff said that didn't apply to them and produced a piece of paper with his father's signature and a bunch of fancy words written by a lawyer. He argued that his father wouldn't deal with lawyers. The sheriff pointed to other signatures, notaries he called them. But he didn't believe it. They'd fabricated that document, he had argued. Thirty days, the paunch sheriff said, thirty days or they'd be thrown out. His mother simply sat in a chair and cried.

If his mother hadn't been so stressed, maybe she'd

have taken better care of herself. He'd tried to help her. He'd taken several after school and weekend jobs to help support them. After being booted from the cabin, they had lived in several rundown apartments, but his mother had become more unbalanced. She had begun smoking and drinking more, exacerbating her emphysema. Eventually she had become too ill to leave the apartment.

Life had funny plans though. Jane Smith had died before his mother. But Jane had never had to live in the foul smelling apartments he and his mom had endured. She'd had a nice home and could afford the medical care she needed. She had never suffered the way his mom had.

He had gone to Jane's funeral, but more to gloat and to see his half-brother suffer than in sympathy. His own mother, though still alive, had spent most of her days in bed. Her breathing had become loud demanding gasps. Her color, as drab and grey as a winter fog, had made her look like a corpse long before she died.

After Jane had died, his half-brother had made the effort to get closer to him, even offering to send him to school. He had arranged to stay with a friend while at school and drive the ninety miles home on weekends to see his ailing mother.

During finals of his second and last year, he'd decided to stay near the school and use his time to study. His mother hadn't told him about the eviction notice she had received. With no place to go, she had begun walking the eighteen miles to the cabin. They found her body along Highway 12.

The day of the funeral he had vowed revenge and had decided he'd take back what should have been his. Now, here he was. Though he had planned it differently, as long as he could get into the cabin long-term, it suited his need. His goal was to have his half-brother try and force him out and then he'd expose him for what he was, cruel and callous.

He looked at the house, the dark windows, like eyes peering at him, reminded him of the work he needed to finish. When he finished boarding up the windows, he began pulling off the sheets his asshole brother had thrown over all the furniture. While placing them in the closet, he found the folded flag. It had been hanging upside down on the wall when their father had been alive. He unfurled the large cloth and hung it up, in its same orientation. He looked at his handiwork with pride.

The upside down U.S. flag, a sign of distress and a symbol to all who believed the government had been compromised, had been the core of The Free Militia. Freedom from the government's oppression sat at the heart of everything he'd been raised to believe. His brother, the pansy ass, had abandoned his father's teaching and believed in the establishment.

*

Mac drove Keeva to work and walked in with her. "Hello!" Lucy called to them, wiping her hands on her apron. "After your phone call this morning, I didn't think you'd be here today."

"I'm not sitting in the apartment all day. I already feel like I'm being hunted like a duck." Keeva, the strain of the night still weighing on her, sat down. She picked up the list of notes, the same ones Tighe left every night.

Lucy pulled them from her hand. "Oh, no you don't. I'm the manager and I'm going to start taking care of some of Tighe's complaints." She put the notes in her apron pocket.

"What is he bitching about now?" Keeva sighed, placing her elbow on the counter and resting her head on her palm.

"Most of it is the same. He does say he can't get into the storage closet." Lucy looked at her. "I wonder what he needs in there?"

"I think he likes extra supplies when he's baking, just in case he needs them. But until I figure out what is going on here, nobody but you and me get in there." Keeva didn't want to think about Tighe or his complaints right now. Other things occupied her mind.

Keeva kept busy working in the dining area. Most days she had very little time to enjoy her customers, but today she had allowed herself the luxury of spending time with them.

Keeva turned when she heard her name called. Rhonda, a regular customer who worked at 9-1-1 dispatch, was hurrying toward her. "Are you all right?" Rhonda pulled her into a tight hug with her ample arms, squeezing the air out of Keeva.

Catching her breath, Keeva stepped back. Behind Rhonda, she saw a young man looking in their direction. He wore a baseball cap pulled low over his face, but she could see his focus had been on her. Something about the way he stared sent chills through Keeva. She turned back to Rhonda. "I'm fine. I'm feeling like Chicken Little. All these little frights and nothing is real."

"But, sweetie," Rhonda grabbed both her hands, smothering them in hers, "you've been through so much. Everyone knows this guy is a monster, you have every right to be worried."

"Thanks, Rhonda. I'm just hoping they catch him soon." Keeva stepped aside to let Rhonda walk to the counter and glimpsed back at the man in the cap. He still followed her with his eyes. If he had been a regular customer she would have known him, but she knew she'd never seen him in the shop before. It bothered her she couldn't place him.

"But you don't have to worry now that Detective Salazar has taken an interest in you." Rhonda nudged her with her elbow and bellowed a laugh that caused almost everyone in the café to look in her direction.

"Rhonda! Where did you hear that? He has not taken any interest in me. He's only around because he's doing his job." Keeva wanted to believe Tony had taken a special interest in her, but knew his only interest was the case, not her.

"Excuse me, girlfriend. But why did he give me *your* home address as his location last night? All night long?" Thank goodness Rhonda had the sense to lower her voice with the last comment.

Keeva darted her eyes around to make sure no one heard. Most of the customers sitting at the nearby tables had gone back to their own conversations, except for the man with the baseball cap. He still stared at Keeva.

"He only stayed to make sure no one came back to the house." Keeva whispered.

"Uh huh. You keep telling yourself that." This earned Keeva a bump from Rhonda's shoulder, nearly knocking her over.

They both chuckled and Rhonda moved away to place her order at the counter. Keeva turned to resume her work and heard the door to the café slam. The table with the man in the cap was now empty.

By closing time, six p.m., some of the stress had dissipated and she felt almost relaxed. Keeva was helping Lucy set up for the next day, when she saw Mac come into the kitchen. "I better lock the doors, any-one is likely to walk in," she teased, offering him a grin.

"Aren't you the cheery one?" He walked over and kissed her on the head. She could feel the cold coming off him. "You ready for a run? Or do you want to go home?"

"No, I need to run. I don't like not being able to come and go as I please." She looked over at Lucy. "Lucy wouldn't even let me walk to E-Zee Accounting, two doors down."

"I said you could go, but only if one of us went with you," Lucy chimed in.

Mac smiled and nodded at Lucy. "I told her not to let you go any place alone." He turned to Lucy. "Thank you."

Keeva rolled her eyes. She did appreciate all the care people were taking, but it had begun to feel like walls were closing in on her. Every fiber in her wanted to get out, to enjoy the fresh air with some time alone. Running and hiking through Capital City and the surrounding areas had always been her stress release. Now, thanks to some asshole she couldn't even walk outside alone. Her muscles felt jittery but she wasn't sure if it was nervousness about the stalker or the anxiety over not having her freedom.

She and Mac kept their run in town, out toward the college, all in flat open area. Mountain lions were common in the hilly areas and they came out at dusk. It wasn't worth the risk to head up into the surrounding mountains this time of night. Most of their run had been in silence with a little light chatter. She knew Mac was letting her set the pace, both in their speed and the need to talk.

As they slowed to a walk several blocks from the café, Mac glanced at her, "How you holding up?"

She knew her brother could read her like a billboard, so she stuck with an honest answer. "Like a yo-yo. One minute I want to kill the son of a bitch, and the next I'm crying like a babbling idiot. If it weren't for you and Tony's support, I'm not sure what I'd do."

"You know his support is more than professional?" Mac looked at her out of the corner of his eye and grinned.

"No, it isn't. He probably thinks I'm some neurotic basket case. God, you should have heard me last night." She remembered her outburst. "Besides, like you said, he probably has a black book filled to the brim." She hoped not, but worried even if he didn't have a long list of girlfriends he wouldn't be interested in her.

He put his hand on her arm, "You are not seeing the picture, Keeve," he often shortened her name. "He looks at you like he's seeing the *Mona Lisa* for the first time."

Keeva rolled her eyes. Men, what did they know? Tony looked at her like she was a cartoon, not a masterpiece. "Oh, please. Don't read into it. Tony is not interested in me."

Mac shook his head and didn't say anything else.

When they got to the café, she grabbed her backpack, a substitute for a purse she didn't like to carry, and pulled out her phone. There had been a text from Tony.

Todd had a procedure. Not able to talk to him and will be here 1 or 2 more days.

It shouldn't bother her, but not seeing him, or having him around made her feel empty and alone.

*

Keeva woke up to the sun shining in her window. She felt refreshed after the first decent night of sleep since the attack in the alley. Happiness had settled inside her. Tony had contacted her, let her know about his delay and that he'd be home today or tomorrow. She figured it was just a professional courtesy, but she liked knowing he had thought of her.

Keeva grabbed her phone from the nightstand and unplugged it from the charger. The yellow folder popped up, another message had come during the night. She hoped it'd be from Tony and pressed the message button. But it wasn't from him. It was from Jimmy.

Found the perp. Call me at the station.

She stared at the phone and instead of feeling the relief she expected, she felt conflicted. She was happy they had found somebody. She could have her life back. It struck her that there would be no more case and no reason to see Tony. A profound emptiness filled her chest. Maybe it would be for the better.

Keeva swallowed back tears and called Jimmy. "Hey, I got your message. What's going on?" Anytime she had to call the police, it brought back memories of dealing with her parents' deaths. Her stomach fluttered nervously. Though Jimmy was a friend, he had never called her before.

She could hear him take a breath and dread filled her. "We have good news." He paused. Keeva blinked. Good news? The words sounded foreign to her. Lately nothing had been good news. "They think they found the man who has been stalking you."

Questions ran through her and she didn't know which to ask first. "Where? How did they find him?"

"There was a fatal car accident last night. But they found notes similar to those that have been left for you in his wallet."

"And they're sure it's him?" She struggled for an appropriate response. Days on end filled with endless worry and stress had nipped at her. In one phone call it all vanished and she had her life back.

"We don't have all the answers right now. He had the notes and had been wearing a dark sweatshirt with a hood." She heard him shuffling something. "We still need to confirm a few things. I thought knowing we possibly have the perp or at least someone involved could help relax you."

"Sure, sure. Thanks Jimmy," she responded quietly, "Thanks for the call." She sat still on the bed and let Jimmy's words sink in. They had found him. Like a tiny orb of light growing larger, a feeling of relief began to swell in her.

Her phone buzzed in her hand and she opened it expecting it to be another message from Jimmy. It was from Tony.

Home, late last night. Heard news, but you still need to stay safe. Just in case.

Keeva appreciated the concern. But with the sudden news of her freedom, a plan to go for a run emerged. With no more stalker, no more police hanging around her house, and no more oppressive cautions from everyone, the invisible chains dropped off her. She smiled.

CHAPTER 7

FOR THE FIRST time in almost two weeks, Keeva began to relax. She debated a morning jog to the café, but had a list of errands that had piled up and would need her car to do them.

Lucy was already at the café when Keeva arrived. "Keeva, did you read the newspaper?" Lucy clapped and was almost laughing as she pointed to the local paper sitting on the counter. The passionate action added to her youthful appearance. With her silky long blonde hair and tiny size, she reminded Keeva of a fairy.

"Jimmy called me. It's great news." Numbness gradually replaced her initial elation. She wanted to feel as excited as Lucy looked, but a wariness still nagged her.

She needed to clear her head and regain some of

her depleted energy. The errands could wait. "Lucy, I need some fresh air and a good long run. Do you mind finishing today? I can come back later."

"Of course I don't mind. But I will mind if you come in. Take the day off. You've been through enough and need a break." She smiled at her. "Maybe you can get that handsome detective to take you to lunch?"

"You sound like Mac. But it isn't like that." It wasn't for lack of desire on her part, but a man like Tony wouldn't give the likes of her more than a passing glance. No, it was not and would never be like that.

She'd jog up Grizzly Gulch. There would be wildflowers up there now. They would be a nice reminder of the beautiful days ahead. Though a bit chilly out, the sun was bright and a big blue sky hinted of summer's arrival.

She felt sluggish at the beginning of her run but as she approached the Walking Mall her adrenaline had kicked in, giving her much needed energy. It was a beautiful Montana spring day, with its clear blue sky that gave Montana its nickname, Big Sky State, and brightened everything it touched. Keeva moved her face up and felt the warmth from the sun radiate down on her face.

A half mile later as the path opened to the library, she saw Tony. His broad shoulders and dark hair made him stand out. Slowing her pace and shortening her stride, she lifted her hand to wave, but instead he was walking in the opposite direction. She stopped unsure if she should call out. As she opened her mouth to speak, he approached a dark haired, slim female, put his hand on her back, leaned over and kissed her cheek. A little boy grabbed his leg. Tony picked him up and hugged him before setting him down next to the woman who was almost as tall as he was. Her stylish white dress contrasted her long dark hair. She was stunning.

The embarrassment of intruding on an obviously intimate moment made her angry with herself. The anger merged with a sense of irrational disappointment. Tony had given her no reason to think he had an interest in her, but she had nursed the foolish hope nonetheless. Seeing him with this woman and child left little doubt he was committed to someone else. She swallowed hard and reminded herself that the first night she'd met him she had known men like Tony wanted beautiful skinny models, not plain outdoorsy women like her. "So be it," she said as she tried to push back a tinge of sadness.

The little boy tugged at the woman's hand, pulling her toward the library's entrance. Keeva tried not to watch the scene, but when Tony and the woman laughed, her gaze whirled in their direction. They appeared to be conversing but they were too far off for Keeva to understand.

She put her head down to avoid any more of the sight and began her run with longer and faster strides. Get over it, Keeva. He had never been anything but professional to her. Still, she couldn't squash her disappointment. She picked up her pace and lifted her head, focusing on the run ahead.

Tony turned toward the movement in his peripheral vision and saw Keeva. She had turned left from the parking lot and was running up Grizzly Gulch. She was about to run beyond the building so he called out to her. She didn't respond and kept running. Already late for work, he tried not to think of those long legs, but his resistance fell apart every time he saw her.

He looked around for Mac but didn't see him in the area. "Damn it," he punched the hood of his car, angry that she had ignored his warning not to run alone. Smith needed to learn to keep his mouth shut. Until they could prove this guy had been the perp and that he had worked alone, Keeva could still be in danger.

Yanking the door open, he dropped onto the seat, starting the car before he had the door closed. He threw the shift into gear and squealed his tires of the Highlander on the asphalt as he backed out of the small parking lot. What the hell was she thinking? She had run right up Grizzly Gulch, a deserted dirt road. With so few houses in the area anything could happen to her.

He honked the horn behind her, watching her jump to the side of the road and turn in his direction. Her hand flew up over her chest. Annoyance crossed her face. Tony pulled up behind her, as far off the dirt road as he could. Stepping out of the car, slamming the door behind him, and taking large strides, he reached her in three.

"What the hell are you doing?" His voice sounded as strong as his heartbeat. He knew anyone could get to her up in the mountains around Capital City. He wanted to throttle her, or at least take her over his knee and give her a good whack.

"I'm jogging, what does it look like I'm doing?"

"You are kidding me, right? You have some creep stalking you and you're out here, by yourself, jogging along a deserted road in the middle of nowhere?" Discretion be damned, he thought.

"I do not have a stalker. They found him. Plus I am not in the middle of nowhere, and even if I was, what I do is none of your damned business!"

"It is my business to keep you safe." Tony stormed to within inches of her. He could feel her quickened breath on him. Beginning to flush and sweat from her run, the odor of sweat mingled with her sweet perfume. His brain told him to back up, but his groin urged him closer.

"Don't pretend nothing is going on, someone might still be following you. I asked you not to go anywhere by yourself and here you are," he swept his arm out wide. "Until we know for sure the man we got was the perp, or what is going on, you need to make sure you have someone else with you."

Keeva stepped back. "You are not my bodyguard."

"Someone needs to watch out for you." His voice trailed off. He could see her chest rise and fall from the run. Her face, flushed and covered with dots of moisture that accentuated her full lips turned belligerent. His anger trailed off as an urge to taste her sweetness began to overpower his irritability.

He leaned over her, edginess and the desire to taste her warring within him. He saw her eyes widen and her lips part as though she planned to speak but he lowered over her, inhibiting any sound with the pressure of his lips.

Keeva's mouth, soft and creamy, tasted like warm caramel. *Dios mio*, he wanted her. Her initial resistance waned, and Tony softened the kiss taking what she offered. She pressed closer to him and opened her mouth when his tongue teased the seam of her lips. His burgeoning cock tightened his pants.

Breaths quickening, their arms wrapped tighter, as they pulled each other closer. Tony felt her passion riveting, gripping him harder before she suddenly hesitated. Placing her hands on his shoulders, she pushed against him and moved away. Her breath came out in pants. "I guess your girlfriend's kiss wasn't enough." The anger in her voice surprised him.

"My girlfriend?"

"Short term memory problems, detective?"

"What girlfriend?" Tony squinted his eyes and shook is head, feeling as though something had happened and he had missed it.

"Let's see, two minutes ago you kissed another woman down by the parking lot. That doesn't sound like a problem to you? It does to me."

Tony's brain kicked into gear and began to comprehend everything. "You mean Mari?" He grinned. She didn't like him with another woman. He liked that.

"If that's her name."

"Mari, about your height, long dark hair, and yes, I just kissed her *on the cheek*." He crossed his arms.

"Sounds about right. Is she your girlfriend or your *wife*? "

He lowered his focus from her sage green eyes to her soft lips. A hunger to taste them again spread through him. His desire to take her on the road, right now almost wrestled a win over his self-control.

He placed his hand behind her neck and said, "No, *chula*, she is not my wife, or my girlfriend. She's my sister."

"Mari."

"Yes, Mari." He arched an eyebrow, "Now, if it

had been my ex-wife, there wouldn't have even been a handshake. And I don't even know her whereabouts so little chance of that. By the way, the only woman I have *really* kissed in recent months is you."

Keeva opened her mouth to speak, but Tony lowered his mouth over hers, brushing his lips across hers. He took her lower lip in his teeth, then he let go and his tongue teased the spot his teeth had grazed. The sweet smell of pine, intertwined with Tony's own masculine scent, sent a twisting corkscrew of excitement through her.

His fingers rubbed the back of her head and sent chills up her spine. He pulled her tighter, pressing harder with his ravenous mouth. Holding her tight, he deepened his kiss. His kiss became demanding, possessive.

A desire for something deeper swelled within her chest. Her breathing had become erratic. She put her arms around his waist, needing to feel him. His body was solid and hard beneath her touch.

His kiss released a passion she had never experienced before. Her desire for him, for more, overwhelmed all rational thought. Her body wanted, demanded his touch. A quiver ran from her stomach to the apex of her thighs.

Tony moved his mouth to her neck, kissing his way to her ear where he nibbled on her earlobe. Prickles and chills pirouetted over her skin. Soft words came from his mouth, "Were you planning to run up the ridge trail?" The breath warming her ear, increased the weakness in her knees.

"Hmmm, I was."

When Tony pulled away, the air between them took on an instant chill. "Didn't you get my text?" he asked holding her by the shoulders and peering down at her. "We are not sure he is the guy, and if he is, there is evidence he worked with someone."

Her voice was weak, still panting, "But Jimmy said…"

He covered her mouth with his finger. "Jimmy should have minded his own business. He only knows what he was told in the report." Tony moved his finger away.

Her eyes searched his, looking for answers, answers he couldn't give her. Tony searched her eyes wanting to know if she comprehended the situation. The situation he had just made worse. He wanted her, he couldn't deny that, but at what cost to her?

"I'm sorry, Keeva. I'll explain as much as I can, but right now there are things I cannot tell you." He wanted to throw her in the car, take her some place safe and get her away from danger. The desire to make love to her was as powerful as the need to protect her. "This whole thing doesn't feel right. There is something too convenient and sudden about it. Even if this is the guy, we have a few reasons to believe he could have had a partner."

Her eyes glistened. He saw her swallow, and she blinked. *Ay, Dios.* He didn't know what he'd do if she began crying. He felt helpless and it pained him to see her hiding her disappointment. She blinked again and the moisture disappeared. A slight sensation of relief flushed through him. She wasn't going to cry, *gracias a Dios.*

A darkening sensation floated over him. The despair that engulfed him caused an emptiness in his chest. Other than his son, family and very few friends, Tony kept his life simple, no commitments or attachments. That same loner defense had kept him sane through countless missions in Delta Force and the CIA. As a trained killer he had survived through violence and an understanding that no one should be trusted. He was used to the sharper edges of life but he worried this soft, sweet smelling, innocent woman would be hurt if she knew his capabilities.

Keeva worried about flour, sugar and keeping employees happy. She wanted to jog safely to work and feed hungry souls. His jaded view on life would drain the energy of her rose-colored world. Beyond ridding her of the evil cretin who could still harm her, he should keep his relationship with her professional. The warm sensation her lips left on his reminded him he had crossed that line.

He walked around the car and opened the door. "I understand this is hard and I promise to do everything I can to straighten it out." She walked over to the car, and sat in it, pulling the door from his hand to close it. After putting the seatbelt on, she looked out the window.

Tony got into the driver's seat. "I can't let you out in the woods alone right now, but how about we go to the woods together. Hiking. This weekend?" He started the car and put it in gear. "I'll check with a friend at the Forrest Service and find out what is open." He turned the car around and headed back toward the café. "Work or home?"

She dropped her hand and looked at him. "The café. I have my car there." She smiled at him but he didn't see sincerity in the smile. "You don't need to keep me company, Tony. I'm sure you have plenty to do other than babysit me."

Glancing at her, he placed a hand on her knee. "I want to do this. We both need a break. And this will give you a chance to meet my son."

"The adorable little boy with you and Mari?"

"Yes. That's my boy, TJ."

"I'd love to meet him. The café is closed on Sunday, does that work for you?"

"It's a date." He gave her a glance and a small smile.

She chuckled. "A date it is."

*

From the view in his car, he watched Keeva leave the café and jog in the direction of the Walking Mall. He rubbed his face, feeling the scratch of a beginning beard.

The police still watched her home and the café, but not as heavily as prior days. He had hoped she'd jog someplace he could approach her, but the Walking Mall, surrounded by businesses and retail stores made it impossible for him to approach her without being seen.

The library was the only place she could exit, unless she turned around. He took the chance she'd come out of the library and run up Grizzly Gulch. He drove over to Park Avenue where he could see where she went when she left the Walking Mall.

He smiled when he saw her turn up Grizzly Gulch. This time of day during the week there was very little traffic on the dirt road. The road twisted through the surrounding mountains, surrounded by tall pine trees and had very few houses. It was a perfect place to get her alone.

An SUV turned up behind her. He recognized the detective from the night she fainted. "Damn it." he wanted to hit something. He had planted the evidence so they would think they had the man that had been after her. Why was he following her? Could his interest be more than professional? He was furious.

He stomped his foot on the car floor and hit his knee on the steering wheel. "Fuck." Pain shot through his knee and leg. He wanted to smash something. The detective's head would be a good start.

If he tried to follow her he'd risked having the detective see him. He had no choice but to sit and wait. It paid off. Less than five minutes later he saw the detective's car drive out. Keeva sat in the front seat. He bristled. What the fuck was going on? He put the car in gear and followed from a safe distance.

He parked a few cars down from the café where the side of the building was still visible from his rear-view mirror.

From this spot, he saw the detective get out of the car and walk around to open Keeva's door. He seethed. How dare he get near her? Then the detective bent down and gave her a quick kiss. A pain burst in his gut as he watched their faces move apart, their hands still holding each other's arms. Blackness engulfed his vision and anger exploded, ricocheting through him like shards of shattering glass tearing through his insides.

He wanted to hurt the asshole detective and hurt him bad. He could almost feel the cold pipe in his hand and hear the sound of the other man's skull breaking, just as Todd's had. Gasping at the thick stale air in the car, he could only manage short erratic breaths. Fighting the anger and panic, he slowly gained some control. Gradually his gasps slowed to deep breaths as he calmed himself.

If he made any crucial errors now, they might find him before he succeeded with his plan. Soon he would have Keeva to himself. Then she would realize they belonged together.

Even his own mother had needed time to understand his father. Keeva would understand their destiny. He had to remain patient.

The police believing the man who had died in the rollover was the one who had left the notes for Keeva was key to him getting close to her. Once they believed she was no longer in danger, then he would be able take her to the cabin. *Their* cabin.

*

Sunday had not come soon enough for Tony. For the last few days, thoughts of Keeva's warm soft mouth had interfered with his concentration. He had planned to pick Keeva up and bring her back to the house to meet Mari before they went hiking.

Tony pulled up to the curb as Keeva came outside. He watched her move, her nylon khaki hiking pants cradling her curvy hips, the tucked-in shirt showed off her slim waist. It was a provocative sight. He felt himself hardening and doubted she knew how seductive she was with the simplest acts.

Reaching the car, she handed him her backpack as she slipped into the seat. He stepped around the back of the SUV, popped the back latch and placed the day-pack inside.

Returning to the driver side of the car, he bent over and looked in. She had already buckled her seat belt. He pulled himself into the seat and turned to her, "Ready? We'll stop and get TJ." She nodded, her fingers pulled at the thigh pocket of her convertible hiking pants. "Something wrong?"

Her lips turned up slightly, and she shook her head. "No, I'm fine. Nervous, feeling stupid." She scrunched her shoulders up. "All of the above." Her chin dipped down, she stared at her fingers that once again had begun pulling at the pockets flap.

Every move she made fascinated Tony. His training taught him to read people, but also to disassociate. You did your job and didn't worry about their issues. With Keeva he cared how she felt. Her feelings mattered to him.

One of his last operations in the CIA had been with Gardiner. For over a year they had used the cover as married journalists writing a series on ex-patriots living overseas in order to expose a world-wide sex trafficking ring. Within several weeks, they had lived like a married couple in the bedroom and out. He liked her, she had been a good friend, but he had been able to separate his personal feelings. At the time he told himself it was what the job required but Gardiner felt different.

"Do you care about anything, Salazar?"

Tony knew it wouldn't end easy, he expected a few tearful hugs, but not the hurt he saw on her face. "What the fuck are you talking about, Gardiner? It's work, a job, not the real thing."

"Unbelievable." Her voice boomed in the tiny Kosovo apartment. "For the past freaking year we have lived together, and you call it a job?" She stormed off to the bedroom. Through the thin walls, Tony could hear her sobs.

Due to Tony and Gardiner's work, they had broken up the sex trafficking ring and Interpol had made the arrests. He and Gardiner were packing up and planning some time off.

Gardiner had wanted them to go to the Maldives and had surprised him with plane tickets and reservations. As part of their assignment, they were supposed to have honeymooned in the Atolls, south of Sri Lanka. To give credibility to their cover, including pictures, before they went to Europe they had spent several weeks vacationing on the islands. She had thought they should revisit, but he had suspected she had wanted to continue the sham marriage.

He had told her no, he was going to Miami to relax in the sun and spend time with his family. Nothing in his plans had included Gardiner.

Tony knocked on the bedroom door before pushing it open. "Hey, I'm sorry. It's been a stressful year, Nala.

I mean, Gardiner. See, I'm still calling you by your op name. Can't you see it's important we step back from all of it? A year as someone else is a long time and it becomes easy to forget who we really are. I can't say what works for you but I need at least a few weeks alone to clear my head."

Gardiner sat up in the bed and wiped her cheeks with the back of her hands. "So none of this," she moved a hand across the front of her, "means anything to you? You can honestly just call it a job? I'm sorry, Tony, but I don't know how to separate what we had."

Tony leaned into the wall and closed his eyes, trying to find the words that would not hurt her more. He opened his eyes and moved from the door frame. Stiffening because he knew whatever he said would cause her emotional pain. "Perhaps before either of us takes another assignment, we can go back to the islands together."

Gardiner had left the apartment later that day. A week later Tony received a call from another agent telling him Gardiner's body had washed to shore after a late night swim off the South Ari Atoll in the Maldives.

So far he had allowed two women into his life. Susie, who became so bitter and angry she wouldn't even acknowledge the son they shared, and Gardiner. The friend he pushed to the brink of despair.

Tony didn't know if Keeva could care for him,

but he was falling for her. These sensations were new grounds for him.

"Why? You are not stupid and you have nothing to be nervous about."

"I know, it's silly, but I'm anxious about meeting TJ and embarrassed about Mari. You know. My faux pas the other day." Her cheeks reddened.

He placed his hand behind Keeva's head and suppressed a smile. "Don't worry, I told her not to point and laugh at you." Her eyes widened. "I'm kidding. You don't have anything to be embarrassed about. I didn't mention your jealousy." He backed up as she playfully slapped him. "I only told her we met through the job and that we were hiking today."

He had kept his hand behind her neck and Keeva leaned into his arm. Tony pulled her closer and placed his lips over hers. He moved his tongue to the slit in her lips and she responded, opening her mouth to his. Kissing Keeva affected him like the first glass of wine, sending ripples of pleasure through his body.

He moved away and they stared at each other. Without a word, he kissed her forehead and focused back to starting the car before things heated up and they didn't get back for TJ.

*

"*Papi, Papi*, I'm ready." He heard TJ long before he entered the room. His son held up a small plastic fishing pole and wore a child's fly-fishing vest and hat.

"*Mira.*" He scooped TJ up and bent his head back to get a closer look at his son. His hair, longer than Tony's *high and tight*, had the same curls, but TJ's eyes weren't dark like his. They were more hazel like his mother's. "The fish will be afraid of the big fisherman coming after them."

TJ's dark eyebrows furrowed. "They won't be 'fraid of me. We don't keep them. *Titi* Mari says we let them go." His voice softened in concern.

"Of course we let them go. But they try and hide anyway. I bet they know they can't hide from you." He smiled reassuring his son. TJ's innocence always awed him. It was so sincere.

"I don't want to keep the fishies. I like watching them swim around." TJ ran from Tony when he put him down. He gathered up his small backpack and placed it on his back. "I'm ready, Papi."

"TJ, Mari, I want you to meet Keeva." Tony reached back and grabbed Keeva's hand, pulling her next to him.

Mari reached out and held Keeva's hand between both of hers. "So you are the one who is managing to get my brother away from work. It's a pleasure to meet you, Keeva."

Keeva gave Mari a smile. "It's a pleasure to meet you too, Mari."

"TJ, this is Miss Keeva."

Keeva bent down and faced TJ, "Hi TJ, it's nice to meet you."

"Hi, Miss Keeba. I like your hair, its curly like sketties." He giggled.

Keeva fluffed her long curls with her hands and laughed with him. "It sure is."

Tony and Mari joined in the laughter. He liked seeing Keeva so comfortable with TJ. Susie had never been comfortable around her own son.

Tony grabbed the child carrier and pack attachment. "I'm not sure when we'll be home," he said to Mari. She leaned against the wall with a *café con leche* in her hand, smiling.

"Have fun. It's nice to meet you, Keeva."

TJ ran up to Mari and she kissed him on the top of his head. "*Pórtate bien.*"

"I'll be good, *Titi* Mari. I 'member everything you tol' me and I'll listen to Papi." He scampered toward the door, running out to the car where he began hopping in circles.

Tony caught up to his rambunctious son. His own restless excitement matched TJ's, though for different reasons. Tony wanted today to be special, for Keeva and TJ to get to know each other. A child of three and a half, TJ saw any outing as an adventure. But an outdoors event inflated into a riveting wilderness expedition in TJ's vivid imagination.

He placed the carrier and pack in the seat next to

TJ. "I don't need that, Papi." TJ pointed to the large carrier he used for longer hikes. "I'm a big boy and can do it myself."

"I know you can, buddy. But just in case you get a little tired, I want to have it. Remember the hike up Mount Helena a few weeks ago?" He had almost left the carrier behind, but had grabbed it at the last minute. TJ hadn't made it a third of the way up the trail when he asked Tony to go in the carrier. "We might not get too far today, but in case we want to, it'll be there."

When they settled in the car Keeva asked, "Where are we going?"

"We are going to Trout Creek Canyon Trail. I wanted to go to Crow Creek Falls but it is still a little early in the season." Tony didn't tell Keeva that Crow Creek Falls was a bit too isolated. He didn't want to take any chances. "My friend that works in the Forrest Service said there is probably still some deep snow along the Crow Creek trail because of the higher elevation. That and TJ wants to fish, and the stream should be running now."

Keeva turned to TJ, "What do you like to catch, TJ?"

"I don't know. I neber caught a fishy before."

Tony listened to Keeva and TJ while he drove out to the hiking area. TJ's mother had left when TJ was so young, he hardly knew her. Tony had never brought any of the women he dated home, so he had worried TJ would be painfully shy, or maybe even angry with Tony bringing home a woman. Keeva's easy-going personality seemed to make everyone comfortable.

They pulled into the parking area and began unloading the car. TJ stood with his plastic fishing pole ready to go. Keeva leaned over to Tony, "He looks adorable in that fishing vest and hat."

He laughed. "That's my sister's doing. He's chattered non-stop about our trip so she took him to Outdoors Supreme and bought it for him." He put the carrier on and grabbed TJ's hand.

"Let's go, sport. Those fish aren't going to wait all day."

"Yippee!" TJ threw his hands up, almost hitting Tony with the fishing pole. His son's exuberance spread warmth through him.

They didn't have to hike far on the flat terrain to get to the stream. Bee lining toward the stream, TJ ran ahead of them. "Whoa," Tony called after TJ with little effect.

Keeva was closer and positioned herself between the stream and the gradual embankment. She turned and put her hand out for TJ to grab hold and helped him to the clearing near the stream. "I have him," she called to Tony. She squatted and began helping him get his pole ready to fish.

"Papi, Papi, Keeba says I might catch a big one." TJ lifted his arms.

Tony silently sucked in a breath, his heartbeat quickening at his son's reckless movement so close to the water.

"Careful, TJ." Keeva put her hand on TJ's arm as she spoke. "You don't want to tumble into the water."

Tony was thankful for her quick response. The stream was rushing fast this time of year, and though it was a few feet from where they stood Tony knew it wouldn't take much to pull him into the cold water. He dug in the pack and pulled out the lifejacket he carried, handing it to Keeva. "Here, we discussed this and he agreed to wear it."

Tony detected Keeva sensed what TJ would do next. TJ clutched the fishing pole tightly in his hand, as Keeva tried to put the life jacket on his wriggling body. She coaxed him to switch hands so she could get the jacket on. Tony sat next to them as Keeva began helping TJ throw his line out. Though he had a plastic pole and fake lure, TJ would never know the difference.

"You're pretty good at this." Tony said to Keeva. He watched as she sat back. She had put on a base-ball cap, her long hair pulled through the back opening, and tendrils hung around her face. The sun's light bounced off her hair making it look more golden than brown. He wanted to run his hands through those curls.

"What, fishing or dealing with children?"

"Both." He had been amazed at how quickly she had anticipated TJ's next move and didn't seem to mind the enthusiasm he put into everything. "You were ten steps ahead of him before I even reacted and you obviously know all about fishing."

"Ha. I deal with kids all the time at the café, so anticipating and reacting quickly is easy." She looked pensive for a moment, but then smiled. "As far as the fishing, I better be. I've been fishing since I was his age. And my dad made us use real lures and fishing poles." She looked at him, and held his gaze, as though she wanted to trust him. Then she smiled as though he had given her the answer she wanted.

He wished he could frame the sight before him. The sun shone on her, accentuating her flawless skin. With her bright smile and the halo of curls, she looked angelic. "The first fish I caught, I was just a little older than TJ, and my mom had to help me reel it in. At my age, it looked like a monster fish to me." She took a slow breath in and pinched her lips. Just a quick movement, but Tony thought he registered sadness on her face. "The thing flopped around so much, I screamed and dropped my pole." A soft laugh escaped from her. Tony liked to see her laugh. She seemed to find the joy in the simplest of events. Soft warmth ran through him at the reminder of her constant kindness. Even a fish hadn't been spared her compassion. He wondered what it would be like to spend most of his time around her.

"It didn't stop you, though." Tony turned on his side and rested back on one elbow, able to watch TJ as he spoke to Keeva. "You obviously still fish." He suspected she succeeded in anything she tried. "My dad had me out again the next week. I finally got the knack of catching the fish. As soon as I was able, I learned to release the fish on my own." She lifted her face toward the sun. The movement caused her flannel shirt to gape. The soft curve of her breast peeked out of the opening in the red plaid. Her skin looked as soft and unblemished as a first winter's snow, making him wonder if she was as smooth everywhere else.

"Dere's no fish here." TJ's impatient voice distracted Tony from his thoughts. "Look." He held up his pole. "Dere's no fish here, Papi. Let's try the big water." He dropped the pole next to Tony, returning to the water's edge. Squatting down, he picked up a handful of smooth rocks rounded by the flowing water. He held up the glistening rocks up for them all to see. "Look, dey have pwetty colors."

Keeva sat up and placed a hand under TJ's tiny hand. "Wow, they look like gems."

"Gems? Can we keep the gems?" Tony watched his son look up at Keeva, his large round eyes trusting, even though he had just met her. Tony had been feeling something for days, but until now he hadn't recognize the trust he had placed in Keeva. Cognizant of his own growing attraction toward her, he was thankful TJ also had accepted her.

"Maybe we can keep just one. The fish live in the water and need the rocks." Keeva's tone was gentle.

TJ liked to collect treasures and Tony knew by the time they got home he'd have all their pockets filled with souvenirs. Keeva looked up at him and Tony winked, mouthing a "Thank you" for her quick thinking.

Tony gathered the fishing pole and took TJ's hand and the three of them began walking down the trail. Keeva and Tony flanked TJ, but about a mile in, the trail narrowed and Keeva moved in front of Tony. Their going was slow with TJ's little steps and his constant stopping to bend down and examine things.

Walking behind Keeva gave Tony a nice view. Her long solid physique glided as the elevation began to increase. With each step, he could see her muscles, tight and long. Her firm round ass moved in a rhythm all its own.

"Papi, I'm tired, can we stop?"

"Okay, buddy." The trio stopped, and Tony looked at Keeva who had already stepped closer to TJ. "Let's let Keeva pick you up and put you in the carrier."

"But I'm a big boy." He pouted. Tony stood firm,

as TJ could be as unmovable as the mountains around them when he wanted. Before Tony could react, Keeva had stooped as close to TJ's height as her five-foot-nine frame would let her.

"In the carrier, you'll be taller than us. You can be our scout. You can look out and tell us if we need to watch out for anything."

"What's a scowd?"

"It's the most *important* job." She exaggerated the word *important*, making sitting in a child carrier sound as exciting as catching those elusive fish. "You will be the one who watches out for everything. Maybe we can see some deer, or elk, and you get to see it first and tell us."

"Impawtent? Like da nice lady at the liberry who sometimes picks me to help her? She says it's impawtent to be still and quiet and hold the book."

"Yeah, like that. Only you can tell us when you see something special." Before she had any further argument from TJ, Keeva had scooped him up to place him in the pack. TJ was built like Tony and was tall and solid for a child his age. Mari had started to have trouble lifting him but Keeva raised him with ease. Tony turned and squatted so Keeva could place TJ in the carrier. At six-three and a solid two hundred twenty pounds, Tony had never been interested in petite or thin women. The women Tony met tended to fit into two categories. They were either wafer-thin or out of shape. Neither type had appealed to him. But not Keeva, she was neither. Built with firm curves that would rival any of Hollywood's 1940's sex sirens.

"There you go. Now remember to look for animals. But don't talk too loud so we don't scare them away. Okay?"

"'kay." TJ responded to the salute Keeva gave him.

With TJ in the carrier, Tony no longer had to stop to wait for him and was able to walk in stride with Keeva. "Have you hiked here before?" he asked.

"Yes, but it's been a few years. We used to camp at Vigilante Campground when I was a kid. Then we'd hike here or head over to Refrigerator Canyon and do a longer hike." The trail narrowed even further, forcing Tony to walk slightly behind Keeva. Their arms would occasionally touch as he leaned in to hear her when she spoke. He felt her hand touch his, warm from the exertion of hiking. Wanting to feel her again, he took advantage of their close proximity and grabbed her hand. She responded, wrapping her fingers around his. It felt good to have her react to him so easily. He stroked the side of her hand with his thumb, wishing he could stroke other places.

"Look, Papi. Dere's a squirrel." Tony watched a squirrel scamper up the tree.

They were looking at the squirrel and Tony felt Keeva's hand move away. He missed the warmth. Simultaneously she signaled to be quiet with her finger over her lips and pointed with the other. She whispered, "Look over there. See in the leaves, there's a fawn." The small animal, curled in a pile of leaves, eyed them cautiously.

"Is dat a baby deer?" TJ tugged on Keeva's shirt. "How come it's got spots all over? Is it sick? Where is the mommy?" he said, his voice loud enough the deer lifted her head higher, it's instincts kicking in.

"The mommy is getting food. She'll be back." Keeva stepped closer to TJ, brushing up against Tony.

When she leaned her head in closer to the carrier, some of her curls fought their way out of the band she constrained them in and brushed Tony's cheek. Their wisps were soft and left a fragrant trail. He longed to bury his face in her hair, inhale the scent and then follow a trail down her neck to the hollow where her shirt gapped.

Bending closer, she whispered to TJ, "The spots are normal. When she gets bigger she'll be all one color." Her breasts pressed against Tony's arm, a sign she wasn't at all aware of what she did to him. The brief contact sent heat to more than his arm and increased his desire to explore beneath her flannel shirt.

"What if her mommy don't come back? Den she'll be 'lone." TJ looked straight at Keeva. "I don't have a mommy, but I have *Papi* and *Titi* Mari." He sounded sorrowful. "I hope her mommy comes back," he whispered.

Keeva faced Tony and she saw him draw a breath. Turning her attention back to TJ, she attempted to reassure him. "She will, TJ, she put her baby in a safe place while she went for food." She took a second glance at Tony but was unable to read any emotion in him.

She placed a hand on his arm and felt his muscle flinch. The concern was clear. How stupid she'd been to point out the lonely looking animal. Most people didn't know fawns in the woods were rarely abandoned, just waiting for their mothers to return. So how could a three-and-a-half-year-old? Her stupidity reminded her how naïve she was in her understanding of children, and worse, how naïve she was to want more from Tony.

The way he'd flinched away from her touch was a reminder of her inexperience. In the future, she vowed to keep her guard up. That and to not be so stupid. She should have guessed TJ was beginning to understand his mother's absence, and she had managed to remind him of it.

"Do you hab a mommy, Keeba?" His voice was so sad it sent a twinge to Keeva's stomach.

"No, I don't." Keeva felt unsure how to answer TJ so she kept it simple. She had thought the fawn was beautiful. Instead, it reminded Tony of his ex-wife and TJ of his lack of a mother. Without even intending it, she managed to hit her targets, but with the wrong kind of arrows.

Tony stepped around her and kept walking with TJ looking back at the fawn from the child carrier. Though the awkward moment passed, it hung in the air.

The birds twittering and the gentle wind through the trees softened the sharpness of the forced silence.

"Look *Papi*, look Keeba. Dere's a mommy deer." TJ clapped in excitement. "I bet dat's da baby's mommy." He looked back at where they had been and smiled at Keeva.

She winked at him. "I bet you're right. And she will be back to her little one in a few minutes." Keeva felt a little relief. TJ had forgotten the issue, but she knew Tony wouldn't forget so quickly.

Tony hadn't known how to react to the whole mother issue. His lack of words only seemed to make the situation worse. But what if he said the wrong thing? The tension when TJ mentioned his mother had been obvious in Keeva's face. A cloud had moved in, blocking the sun, darkening the bright day, the jade green pines and Tony's mood.

They stopped to let TJ try fishing again where the stream reappeared. From there they continued hiking the few miles until they reached the turnaround spot.

"My tummy's growling."

"I can hear it, you're going to scare all the animals."

Tony smiled and reached around, tugging his son's leg that dangled from the backpack. "We'll stop up ahead and eat. I saw some nice rocks near the water," Tony answered.

Tony pondered what to say to Keeva. The rest of the hike had appeared to go without incident, but a spear of tension still ripped through the atmosphere. Keeva had been quiet except for her interactions with TJ and a few words to Tony.

If there was a way to go back in time he would. He should have spoken up and softened the whole encounter. He probably should have explained the whole situation to Keeva beforehand so she'd be aware of the sensitive issue. But he had never been very good at communicating and probably would have screwed it up anyway. He always did.

They stopped at the clearing and sat on some flat rocks. The cloudless sky and bright sun had brightened the mood. Keeva pulled food from the back pack but never looked at Tony. Instead she focused on placing the items out on the flat rock they were using for a table. "Do you like peanut butter sandwiches, TJ?" She had begun unwrapping one.

"Dat's my faybrit." He bounced on his bottom as Keeva placed the open sandwich and a boxed juice next to him. TJ moved off the rock and squatted on the ground. He pulled the rocks he collected earlier from his pocket and began moving them around the food, as a car would maneuver around a track, making noises to match.

Tony had pulled out a wipe and washed off his hands. "Eat first and play later."

"Yes, *Papi*." TJ picked up his sandwich and took a bite.

She pulled out several more sandwiches, handing one to Tony, but still not making eye contact. He felt like a tongue-tied thirteen-year-old, grunting, "Thanks." He opened the foil to find his favorite, a Cuban sandwich.

"My favorite," Tony declared.

"I took a guess. And I hope I got it right." Her response was subdued. He marveled at her talents.

She placed the sliced apples and some chocolate chip cookies on the makeshift table. The latter earned a squeal from TJ. She had asked Tony about TJ's favorite foods, but she'd never asked what he liked. She had managed to please everyone. And all he had done was screw it all up.

The earlier incident wore on Tony, enough that mid-bite he pulled his sandwich away from his mouth. He looked at TJ who was occupied in his food and watching the water. "Hey, about before," he spoke quietly to Keeva. "TJ doesn't understand death or I don't think he does. I should have explained to him about the fawn's mother being nearby. " He waited, unsure how to say the next words. "I'm sorry about

x

your mother, I wasn't sure. Jimmy had said something the first night about it just being you and Mac."

Keeva looked at him, he could read the sadness in her large green eyes. "It's okay. It's been four years. I guess it's something I'll never get over." The pain in her voice struck Tony.

"TJ is pretty protected. For the longest time he never asked about you-know-who, and when he does, he dismisses it with any explanation we give him. I took him to a counselor who told me he'd ask when he was older and saw a difference between himself and other kids. With Mari there he seems less concerned about who's missing."

"It's good he has you and Mari." She smiled at him. "He has enough love so he doesn't feel the neglect. I bet you've seen enough to know sometimes having both parents doesn't mean everything is perfect."

Tony placed the sandwich on the wrapping and stared at his son who had resumed playing with the rock. "Yes, I do." They ate in silence.

"Can I ask what happened to your parents?"

She had begun packing the trash and didn't look up at him. "It was a car accident. Four years ago, but some days it feels like yesterday."

Tony reached over and stopped her busy hands. She looked up at him and he held her gaze. He spoke six languages fluently and could converse in several others but had trouble finding the words to express his emotions in any of them. Like a whip seizing hold, in an instant he understood he wanted to know all about her. "I'm here if you need to talk about it."

When they had finished clearing everything and Keeva replaced the trash in a bag in her pack, Tony said, "Okay sport, it's time to go."

"'kay, *Papi*."

Tony tried to lift him into the carrier, but TJ pulled his arm away.

"I wanna walk. I need more things. Mari likes me to show her things I find owside." TJ dashed ahead of Tony before bending down to peer at something on the trail. "It's a pinching bug!" TJ hollered. He jumped up and moved behind Tony.

Keeva bent over it and picked it up. Both Tony and TJ backed away.

"It's only the shell of a stag beetle," Keeva said, holding the bug toward them.

"Will it bite me?" TJ leaned around Tony's leg and stepped closer. Tony didn't feel as brave as his son and held his position.

"No, it's just the outside. The bug isn't in it anymore." Keeva placed the bug in the palm of her hand and slid it closer to TJ, who now looked intently at the creature.

"Papi, come see." TJ picked it up.

Tony shivered, how could anyone touch a bug? "I can see it from here."

Keeva's eyes widened, "You're afraid of bugs. A big guy like you," She chuckled.

Tony felt his cheeks heat. But he didn't care. Seeing her laugh and relax was worth a joke at his expense. He had missed their easy rapport.

"Shhh." TJ put his fingers to his lips and in a loud whisper said, "Yes, *Papi* is scared of bugs. Mari says don' tell nobody."

"I am not. They just carry germs and I don't like them." He crossed his arms and tried to pretend he was stoic, but couldn't help laughing along with Keeva and TJ. It didn't get him any closer to the bug though. He had always hated creepy crawlies of any kind. It was a fear that had increased after he lived in the Middle East desert where he had encountered gargantuan-sized bugs. He would shake out any of his gear that sat on the ground and on more than one occasion, some monster bug would fall out. The shivers reappeared, running the length of his body as he re-envisioned some of the ugly things.

Keeva placed the bug back on the ground. "We'll leave this one here. We don't want to scare your father, do we TJ?" She gave Tony a grin, and like a derailed train put back on track, he felt the easiness between them reestablished.

"No," he said with a giggle. TJ pointed at the ugly insect, "See, *Papi*, Keeba put down da bug. You don' hab to be scared." With that pronouncement,

TJ grabbed Keeva's hand and the two began walking down the trail.

Tony hurried to catch up, taking one quick look back. "Eww," he mumbled to himself.

They reached the end of the hike a short time later and just in time, too. TJ had become tired, but didn't want the carrier, insisting Tony carry him the rest of the way until they reached the car. He fell asleep five minutes after they drove from the trailhead.

Tony pulled up in front of Keeva's apartment, content that the tension that had been present had shifted. If she were going to be part of their lives, they would have to work out what they told TJ about his mother's absence.

Keeva as part of their lives? The thought surprised him. But he knew he wanted to see more of her. Hell, he wanted to do a lot more than see her.

"Thanks for a great afternoon." Keeva broke into his thought.

"It was my pleasure. Thanks for lunch. You'll have to tell me the secret to the Cuban sandwich. I haven't had one that good since Miami." Tony stroked her forearm as he spoke.

Leaning over, he pressed a kiss to her warm velvety lips. The chaste kiss caused a contraction to pull at his abdomen. Her gaze intensified when he moved away. Her half-lidded eyes told him she felt the same attraction he did. The desire to have more, to pull her closer, deepened.

There was a sleeping sigh from the back seat.

Tony's tense aroused muscles melted like Jell-O when he heard TJ. He pulled back. "I guess our timing isn't the best."

Keeva sighed. "I'll say." She gave him a dreamy smile and he wished he could stay with her. Another sigh from TJ reminded him why he should leave.

*

The next two days were non-stop for Keeva. Sunday's were usually set aside for any bookkeeping work or ordering she didn't get to during the week. After their hike, she had been too distracted to concentrate on much so she had picked up a pizza and a growler of beer and had spent the evening watching movies with Mac.

The café had been busier than usual on Monday, which forced her to spend Tuesday holed up in her office playing catch up. She hadn't even checked her phone until Lucy poked her head in around five.

"Hey, are you still alive in here?" Lucy asked as she plopped a tall glass of diet soda on the desk next to Keeva's computer.

Before responding to the gesture, Keeva began sucking on the tall refreshing liquid. "Thanks, Luce. I was so far behind. I didn't get a damn thing done on Sunday and now I'm paying the piper." She downed more of the cool drink, having to suck in air when she finished.

"And when were you going to spill the beans about Sunday?" Lucy flopped down on the bed that occupied the small office-bedroom. "Mac told me you had a date with Mr. *Hot* Detective, or should I say *caliente*?"

"Calm down. It was a hike with his three year old son, so it wasn't a date," Keeva said. Her dating life had been close to non-existent lately and it embarrassed her to talk about it.

Her back to the wall, Lucy fluffed some pillows behind her. "Come on, Keeva. Mac said you practically gushed about him."

"I did not. You know ever since our parents died Mac gets overprotective if I even mention a guy's name."

"Keeva…" Lucy tipped her head and widened her eyes. Keeva knew this was Lucy's way of saying she didn't believe her.

"Okay, okay. It was a kind of date." Keeva remembered the kiss when he took her home and felt her cheeks blush. "And it was wonderful. Except when his son mentioned he didn't have a mother and I didn't know what to say. It was awkward."

Leaning over her now drawn up knees, Lucy wrapped her thin arms around her slim legs. Keeva held back a sigh. Could Tony have an interest in her?

She wasn't model thin, and her hair took on a life of its own no matter how she fixed it. Mac always told her men preferred women with curves, but he was her brother. Of course he would say things that made her feel better. She could still hope.

Until today, she would have included the business in the unobtainable dream with all the money problems, but in the last few weeks, things had changed. There seemed to be a drop in the expenses and several large standing orders had come back after leaving the business. Something about the sudden timing of everything bugged Keeva, though she couldn't grasp it. She'd have to think about the yo-yo changes in the bakery later in the week and maybe even talk to the Vendors and see what had changed.

"Keeva, give. What happened that made things weird?"

"It wasn't much. You know me and wildlife. She shrugged. I pointed out a fawn and TJ, that's Tony's son with …. He is such a smart little guy and he immediately asked where its mother was and compared it to his own absent mother."

"Oh, shit, I'm so sorry."

"Let's just say it was uncomfortable." Keeva felt like a band suddenly tightened around her chest when she remembered how upset Tony had looked. She knew they worked through it, but what if she continued to say the wrong things? Would he dump her?

Lucy's mouth spread into what Mac called a shit-eating grin. "He didn't look too upset a few minutes ago. He must have gotten over it."

Keeva's eyes widened at Lucy's unexpected comment. "What do you mean? He was here?"

Lucy pushed off the bed and stepped to the door, opening it before turning to Keeva, "Still is. I left him with our two newest hires, Mandy and Hailey, who are probably tripping over each other to bring him his order." Lucy extended her hand signaling Keeva to precede her out the door.

Keeva jumped up, "Why didn't you tell me he was here, like when you walked in?"

"Because then you would never have given me all the juicy parts of your date." Lucy smiled shamelessly.

Brushing past Lucy, Keeva hurried to the stairs but stopped and took in a deep breath. It did little to help. Her stomach still seemed to be doing cartwheels.

She managed to enter the dining room without stumbling. Tony was the only customer. Mandy and Hailey stood behind him, like giggling royal subjects awaiting their next command. His hand half covered his face, looking less regal and more embarrassed.

Keeva moved to the table. "Hello, Tony." She turned to the girls. "Why don't you go in the back and see what needs to be done before closing." They hurried off, tittering and whispering to each other.

Relief washed over his face. He stood. "Hi. I didn't

mean to just drop by without calling but…" His face lit up in a bright smile that made his tanned face even more handsome.

"It's okay. This *is* a café so you can come by for coffee or pastries anytime."

Tony smiled. "Good to hear. Anyway, I wanted to talk to you in person and left a few messages on your phone. I figured you were too busy to call back so I stopped by."

"Didn't even check my phone, sorry. I've been swamped. Business picked up the last few weeks and some of our larger orders that had cancelled have suddenly reappeared. It's all caught me off guard and I'm playing catch-up with all the work." Keeva shook her head, still baffled by the sudden starts and stops in the business. "But anyway, here you are. I hope you are going to give me good news."

"Yes," he paused, "It's good," Tony replied.

"I'm listening." She sat across from him at the table.

Tony stirred the coffee in front of him. "Forensics came back from the notes we found in the accident victim's wallet and they matched the notes you received." His voice flat, contrasted the news.

"I feel like that's good news, but I don't hear that in your tone."

"I can't argue with the forensics. I guess I wish we had more, or at least had him alive." He pulled out two photographs from an inside jacket pocket and slid them across the table.

Keeva leaned over to get a closer look, afraid to touch them. Her palms began sweating. She rubbed her hands together, hoping Tony couldn't tell what a coward she was. *They are just pictures* she tried to tell herself. She pointed to the closest one. It looked like an identification picture. "In this one, he looks a little, I don't know, maybe heavier, and maybe older." She grabbed the next picture. She wondered if it had been Photo-shopped. It had the same man in low lighting wearing a black hoodie pulled up.

That one looked like the attacker. But something was off, she couldn't place it. It did ease her tension knowing they were confirming he had been her stalker. She wondered if knowing he had died made it easier. "This one," she pointed to the second picture, "looks pretty close. But, I don't know." She picked up the picture and held it in front of her face.

The fear and panic she anticipated would overwhelm her didn't happened. "I guess I expected to freak out when I saw his picture. His eyes looked so frightening, but in this, they look normal.

Tony leaned forward, moving the cup to the side. "You aren't sure then?"

She shook her head. "It looks like it could be him. I only saw him a split second both times, and it was always dark."

She returned the pictures. Tony looked at the pictures before pocketing them. The breath he let out and tense facial features expressed his disappointment.

"Sorry, I can't be of much help." Keeva replied.

He put the pictures in his pocket. "The chief is going to hold a press conference in the morning. Everyone believes this is the attacker and probably your stalker. All I have is my gut and that isn't evidence." He blew out a breath. "I spoke to an FBI profiler and he fits the profile, except for the age. He's had family issues his whole life, his wife left with the kids recently and he had lost his job." He shook his head slightly as he spoke.

"But you don't believe it's him?"

"It all points to it being him. I don't know, maybe," he paused, "maybe I just wanted a live person to answer questions, to confess." The last words sounded more like a statement to himself. "It's over and that's what counts." A small smile crossed his face. It looked contrived.

Over. She knew someday there would be no more excuses to see Tony. Keeping her safe had been a job. She didn't need his protection anymore, so he'd have no more reason to see her, to show concern. A void filled Keeva's chest and she felt like she couldn't breathe. She didn't want him to see her so out of control and forced herself to breathe normally. Perhaps he had a bit of a conscience and had figured out she thought more of him than he did of her. How embarrassing. He must be aware of her attraction and now he was trying to let her go easy. There would be no easy way out of this for her.

"So that's it, it's over?" An ache filled the emptiness in her chest. She felt tears pressing at her eyes, the pitfall of falling for someone. It always ended badly. She couldn't let him see what a blathering idiot she might become and managed to blink back the pressing tears.

"Yes. The case looks closed." He surprised her by reaching over for her hand. "You know, with the case solved, you're no longer a witness." It almost sounded like a questioned. Tony's eyes twinkled and his lips curved up.

"Um, yes, I guess."

"That means I won't be seeing you as often." He kept staring at her and his smile returned, "for work anyway."

"What do you mean?"

"I mean I need to find an excuse to see you, and since you aren't a witness anymore, I can *officially* ask you on a date. We can start with a case closed celebration."

Tony's hypnotic eyes focused on her and feathery tingles ran through her arms. She knew she should say no. She should go back to focusing on her business. She'd proven she could say the wrong things, what if he got tired of it? But a night relaxing without fear sounded pleasant. Anything around Tony was fun, and sexy.

"I think that sounds like fun." Keeva flashed a weak smile. She knew spending the evening alone with him would be perilous. It was like agreeing to canoe level-six rapids. Dangerous.

"I still owe you a dinner. Mari took TJ to a friend's in Bozeman for the night so I'm free tonight. I know it's last minute but...." He tipped his head, pouted and used his eyes to plead.

The look was irresistible and she let out a soft laugh. "I'm almost finished but I need a shower." That look, she could look at that face and do nothing else. She sighed inwardly, she knew she was falling for him.

"That's fine. Since I didn't get a chance to cook you a proper meal last time, I should cook for you." Tony weaved his fingers through hers and squeezed. "Your place or mine?" His eyebrows lifted.

She rolled her eyes. "You're incorrigible. I have some elk steaks already thawed. I'll write a few things down, if you could pick them up, and meet me about seven." Keeva pulled her hand away and stuck it into her pocket, struggling to avoid continued contact with Tony. His touch left her feeling vulnerable and unglued.

Tony left through the front door, and she heard the stairs creak. "Lucy, you can come down now."

Lucy bounded down the stairs, shrieking like they were freshmen in college again, giving Keeva a hug. "I'm sorry, I didn't mean to pry, but I had to. Dinner at your place with the sexiest man around, they can't make up stories like this."

"I don't know, Luce. Do you really think he's interested? I'm such a bumbling idiot sometimes. What if it's just trying to say goodbye, you know, case over and moving on?" Keeva wanted to enjoy the dinner and vowed she'd put her worries aside.

Lucy put her hand on Keeva's arm. "Seriously? If he wasn't interested, he'd take you to a bar for drinks not a homemade dinner. I think it's the end of the case and the beginning of something else."

Keeva appreciated her friend's encouragement. She wanted more from Tony and had begun to believe he had a little more than a professional interest in her. "I hope you're right, Luce." She smiled.

"Well, why don't you do more than just hope?" Lucy said with a sly smile.

CHAPTER 8

TONY PARKED IN front of Keeva's place. A fervent desire to spend time with her, conflicted with his normal detached demeanor. Getting deeply involved had never been one of his goals. Until now, he had been fine with keeping all women at a distance. Thinking about her or thinking about being with her had become a preoccupation. He swallowed and pulled himself from the car.

Grocery bags hanging from his arm, Tony rang the doorbell. Keeva answered and offered a slight smile that sent an alarm signal to his intuition. Something was bothering her. He wrestled with whether to inquire about it or just let it be. Once again words failed him.

"Your personal shopper, Madame." He bowed and offered the bags.

"Submission looks good on you." She laughed, grabbed several of the bags and led him to the kitchen.

He breathed in the familiar exotic vanilla scent that hung in the air when she moved away. He helped her unpack the groceries and watched as she began to cook. She looked beautiful. Her unruly hair, like fuzzy corkscrews framed her face. It highlighted her creamy silky skin and high cheekbones. She had on a pair of tight jeans and sweater that looked sexy as hell. But then he suspected she could wear a plastic grocery bag and still look good.

"It already smells good in here. What are you cooking?" Tony asked.

Keeva dipped a spoon into a pot on the stove. Her full plump lips tantalizing as they formed a circle and she blew onto the hot thick red liquid. She held it out for him to taste.

"This is a port reduction sauce. It has port, balsamic vinegar and cherries," she said. "The secret is a high-quality port."

Not too sweet, it tasted like a culinary aphrodisiac. She even cooked seductive. He wasn't sure they could make it to dinner.

"Can I help?" he asked.

"You can get some glasses and pour us each one of those beers you brought. Or I have wine or juice if you prefer something else." She took two steaks out of the oven and placed a thermometer in one. "The glasses are behind me, just to my left."

The small kitchen, an L-shaped wall of cabinets with a peninsula between the cooking area and living had not been built for two people. Someone with Tony's build left even less room for anyone else. Keeva stood at the stove and when he turned to place a glass next to her, she was inches from him.

He leaned in, smelling the rising steam. The aromas were scintillating. Standing this close to her destroyed his resistance. He breathed in the dinner, closing his eyes to see what his senses could discover without looking. He wanted to do the same to her neck but thought better of it. "Hmmm, so enticing." He meant her, but the food smelled good, too.

"I hope you like it." She turned and looked at him.

Her breasts touched him in the crowded space. He could have leaned back a bit. She had the stove behind her, he had some room, but he didn't move.

Her eyes glistened and she surprised him by kissing him. Just a quick peck on his mouth. Her full lips were pillow soft and irresistible. "Detective Salazar, you are distracting. Are you aware of that fact?"

Tony placed his arms around her waist, pulling her into him. He felt himself becoming hard and knew she had to feel the effect she had on him. "It's a detective secret. Disorient them, and then they slip up." He placed his mouth over hers. She responded with equal pressure, moving her lips with his.

Keeva pulled back. "We're about to ruin two very good steaks. How about we eat, and then you can continue to show me your strategies."

As soon as she moved away, he wanted to pull her back. A cold shower was what he needed. It was going to be a long meal.

*

Tony picked up the last plate and dried it. Keeva made him feel so comfortable, he shared more about himself than he had with any of the other women. The darker things he didn't talk about. She would be frightened off if she knew everything. He didn't lie in telling her he was a linguist with the CIA and translated. He just didn't tell her he was a field agent or how he got people to speak the words he needed to translate.

"That was an amazing steak. I'm not usually a fan of game meat, but it didn't taste gamey at all," Tony commented as he put away the plate. "Was that blue cheese you put on before the port sauce?"

Keeva carried the leftovers to the refrigerator, opened the door and placed them inside. "It was a blue cheese butter I made. The secret is in the marinade though. Good cooking requires," she turned from the refrigerator door and smiled, and her eyes took on a sparkle, "some preparation." She paused, her eyes still teasing him. Her lips curved into a slight smile. "Like foreplay."

If he'd had the plate in his hand, he would have dropped it. She increased the whole effect by grabbing a pie from the refrigerator, and in one motion, she plucked a spoon sitting on the counter and scooped up some of the whip cream that decorated the pie.

Her eyes still frisky, she stuck her tongue into the whipped cream and began licking it, leaving a small dollop on her top lip. The lids of her eyes lowered as she pulled the spoon down and licked the whipped cream off her lip with her tongue. He had never seen anyone make food so sensual.

Keeva had not intended to seduce Tony, but it was now or never. The idea, although first insinuated by Lucy, had come to her as she'd rushed to get ready. She would have to admit, though never to him, this was her first rodeo. Well, maybe she'd played with fire, but never had been the instigator. And comparing the guys she dated before with Tony would be like comparing a spark to a flame.

He was so damn comfortable with himself. Suave and secure somehow were all bundled in a bulk of muscle. The men she'd been with were barely out of boyhood.

The closest she'd ever come to a long-term relationship had been with Reggie. And that had been mostly flirting and sexual innuendos in letters and e-mails. Before they could explore where they would end up, he'd been killed in Afghanistan.

Tony hinted at an interest in her, but like shadows seen in the dark, his hints had been vague and elusive. Not like Keeva and Reggie, gushing words of lust to each other over the Internet. Maybe it wouldn't turn into something with Tony, however, she was sure of one thing. She never wanted to regret not taking a risk. Life was too short, too unpredictable to play it safe.

Tony walked over to the couch and sat. He stretched back, one arm extended casually over the back of the couch, while he crossed one leg over the other knee. He oozed maleness and she intended on exploring him. "You want some dessert?" She teased and dipped the spoon into the pie and pulled out more whipped cream.

"No, *chula*," he said. "But I don't mind watching you with that spoon." Hunger filled his half-lidded eyes and he looked like he would like to devour her. The corners of his mouth turned up in a small smile, just enough to let her know how much he was enjoying the scene.

Quivering sensations radiated through her. She stroked her tongue up the spoon, gliding it across her teeth. With the pie in one hand and the spoon held up in the other, she strolled over to the couch, placing them both on the coffee table. As unhurried as she could be, she sat down next to him.

Tony leaned over and began nibbling her ear, "You are all I need for dessert." His tongue glided over the sensitive part below her ear, he followed it by lightly taking her earlobe between his teeth. She closed her eyes to absorb the sensations of his mouth.

Keeva gasped, her whole body felt like jelly, and the tingle she felt between her legs reinforced her decision to have him tonight. No man had ever made her feel the way Tony did. His wonderful seductive tongue touched her just soft enough to offer promises of more.

His kiss succulent, his lips soft, and his velvety mouth on hers felt good. Her instinct took over and she began kissing back, her tongue meeting his. Tony's hand slid down her side, his fingers moved to the top of her jeans, his fingers rubbing between the fabric and her skin, just at the top, teasing enough to make her breath quicken. The area between her legs throbbed with each passing tease. Keeva responded, her pelvis moved against him.

Keeva grasped that she had succeeded in her plan and it startled her. It was as though a distant thought, a faraway fantasy, had become reality. Earlier it had been a picture in her head. It had been an idea, a plan. Now the man she had dreamt about, the man she had begun to fall in love with, the man who she didn't think loved her back, had fallen for her seduction. Reality met fantasy, but all the illusions had been stripped away. He was palpable, he was rock solid, not a hope or a maybe, but there, real, and he was about to undress her. She stilled.

"Don't stop, *chula*." His voice was husky and as seductive as his movements. He ran his hand up her back. "You are *sooo*...remarkable." He pulled her closer, deepening his kiss.

The aching desire throbbing at the apex of Keeva's thighs increased. His passionate reaction to her hesitation deepened her need to want more of everything he did. She heard herself groan and moved with the rhythm of his hips. His hand moved under her sweater and he unclasped her bra. He quickly found her hardened nipples and playfully rubbed at their sensitive tips.

She bit at his lower lip, and the sensation of his large warm hand on her breast sent a passionate vibration through her. She bit his lip hard. He chuckled, "I like when you play rough." Heat ran up her face.

"Sorry," she whispered.

He began kissing the side of her neck. "Mmmm, no apologies needed. I love how you respond." His deep timbre sounded thick. "I want to spend the night." It was a statement, not a question.

A searing desire combined with electrifying tingles

spiraled over her limbs. "Mmh, hmm." Her voice sounded as docile as she felt.

Tony bent, kissed her again and she let out a soft groan, arching back, lifting her hips toward his. Pushing up with his hands, he stood, leaving her to feel the place he had just vacated.

Reaching for her, Tony pulled her up, and without speaking, led her into the bedroom.

The night had turned out much differently than Tony had planned. Keeva had surprised him with her playfulness. He could see in her face she wanted more and it had caught him unprepared. Could she really desire him? Things had gotten so awkward on the hike he had been surprised she had even agreed to dinner.

There had been no doubt what she aimed for in her seductive play, but then she had become shy. For a few seconds Tony had wondered if she had changed her mind. As intoxicating as she looked, he figured she had more men interested in her than she wanted. But there was an innocence to her reactions, as though she was unsure what to do next. The innocent seductress tempted him and he planned to explore that side of her further.

Even if Keeva didn't want a relationship with him, he wanted her to remember tonight. He slid his hand down her back, and she tilted her head up and groaned. Sliding from her lips, down her neck, he kissed the soft sweet-smelling skin she bared.

Tony's own hypersensitive skin tingled as she moved her fingers across his shoulders and up into his hair. He pulled up her sweater, hating to break their contact but the clothes were in the way. She slid the open bra off and dropped it on top of the sweater he had let fall to the floor.

Tony kissed her nipple and it hardened at his soft touch. His erection throbbed and ached in his jeans, but he wanted to go slow. He wanted to please her. He opened her jeans and slid them down. She helped by kicking them off. Her purple and black silk lace panties highlighted her smooth pale skin.

As Tony suckled her nipple, Keeva began unbuttoning his shirt. He helped her with the buttons and discarded his shirt.

Her hands shook as she began unbuttoning his jeans, but she pushed his hands aside when he tried to help her. "No, you don't. This is mine." Her fingers moved so gently, and the act took longer than it should. It teased him, even though he doubted teasing had been her intent.

"You're killing me." He groaned the words.

Finally opening the button, both hands working on the zipper, she leaned in to brush her lips against his. Her full voluminous breast pressed against his chest. "Not a bad way to go." They both chuckled.

Keeva opened the zipper and slid his pants over his hips. Her eyes widened when she saw he had gone commando. He gave her a grin and shrugged, "One less thing to worry about." He kicked off his shoes, and effortlessly removed the jeans along with his socks.

She began to take off the lace underwear, and he placed a hand on her arm, stopping her. "No, keep them on. I want to do that." Naked, except for the dark lace, she went from innocent girl to vixen.

Tony placed his hands on her hips and urged her to the bed. Keeva stepped and laid across the down comforter. He took in the sight, from her curly hair splayed over the pillow to the tips of her polished toes. She looked like a goddess. Her eyes followed his while she bit on the side of her lower lip. Using his outstretched arms to keep his weight off her, he moved his hips between her legs. His erection moved to the heated space at the apex of her thighs. His own body's temperature rose. Her breath hitched, and he could read concern in her eyes. "Don't worry, I won't hurt you."

He gently brushed the tip of his tongue along her lips before pressing down on her lips, coaxing her for more. She responded by matching his pressure, dueling with his tongue while her body squirmed under him. She parted her legs further and reaching around his lower back pressed him closer to her.

He nipped on the pink tip of her breast, and the purr she released told him she had enjoyed it. He flicked the nipple with his tongue and felt her legs contract.

Her breathing increased, but not as much as his own heartbeat. Sex had always been a release for him. He enjoyed pleasing women and he was good at it. But it had never mattered to him if they treasured the memory. This time he cared. The growing need to please her was as shattering as any orgasm.

He slid down, kissing her sweet skin, opening her thighs, gently tickling their delicate insides with his tongue, and finally kissing a trail to the purple lace. "Mmm, you are so soft," he whispered.

Keeva contracted, almost sitting up. Tony pressed a hand to her soft round stomach, "*Calmate, chula*. It's okay. Trust me, tonight is all yours."

Moving the lace aside with one finger, he parted her soft folds and felt her slick sensitive opening. She opened her thighs in response to his touch. Tony moved his fingers into her entrance and placed his mouth over her now engorged clit, licking the sweetness with his tongue. The sweet succulence invigorated his craving.

Keeva inched up, "That is," she wriggled, "amazing."

Tony put a hand under her firm ass and pulled her back. "No escaping now. I always finish what I start." Rubbing one finger between her skin and the lace he stroked the area just above her mound.

"Not fair. You're torturing me."

"And I plan to keep it up all night." He gave her his best wolfish grin. He could almost feel her eyes rolling at his play on words. But they were words he meant. He slid the silky lace panties down her legs and tossed them onto the floor.

Keeva mumbled something incoherent as he continued licking and sucking her. She was so hot and sensitive, Tony had to suppress his own urge to thrust inside her. He slid a second finger to join the first.

"Oh," she whimpered as she writhed. God, he loved to hear her moan. This was Keeva's time and he wanted to please her.

Keeva moaned and trembled, all her muscles tightening. Tony knew she was reaching her peak. Her noises were visceral, increasing his craving for her. He kissed and licked, lifting her solid ass. His muscles tightened as her hips jolted. "Tony," she pleaded. Her back arching, she begged again. "Oh, please." Her muscles squeezed, holding his fingers captive until her spasms began their slow descent.

Tony didn't think he could hold out much longer. He put on the condom he had placed nearby and moved over her. He placed his rigid erection between her legs, her slick opening still pulsated gently.

"You are *so* beautiful," he said and kissed her hard.

Keeva's cheeks glowed pink, highlighting her hungry sage green eyes. Her chest rose and fell with the breaths she panted. He eased his swollen erection a little more deeply into her tight, slick opening.

"Is that okay?"

"Yes, yes." She whispered harshly.

Tony's desperate need drove him deeper into her. He wanted to go slow, to give her a second round of pleasure, but desire to be inside her pushed him forward. He was too close.

Keeva tensed but wrapped her legs around him. She felt tighter than he had expected and he heard her gasp. Her fingers dug into his back and she lifted her hips. He quickened his rhythm and she pulled tighter against him. A small sob escaped her throat.

She was tight at first, but then she relaxed and followed his rhythm. "That's it, baby, move with me." A pounding began building in Tony's groin and he knew he was going to explode. He squeezed his eyes shut and drove deeper into her. Her rhythm now synchronized with his.

Her muscles loosened and he thrust harder, driving into her and building to the rapture he craved. It was too soon, he wanted this moment last longer. But he threw his head back and thrust deep in her. As though on fire, his body blazed with heat and sweat ran off him. An onslaught of intense pleasure pulsed his groin and his release came strong. He collapsed on top of her.

Panting and trying to still his own rapid breaths,

he lifted his head and looked at Keeva. A tear slid from her eye.

Guilt poured through him. He should have been gentler. "What's wrong?"

Her tight pinched lips contradicted the shaking of her head. He withdrew from her, and looked down between them. His still-hard shaft dripped with a pink tinge mixed with her secretions. His eyes flew open and he looked at her.

"You were a..." He couldn't get the words out.

Keeva wiped her eyes with the back of her hand. "I'm sorry. Did I do it wrong?"

Tony froze. "No. No, um. I didn't expect..." Words failed him. That was the best sex he ever had but he felt like a heel not knowing she was a virgin. "No. It was me." He was so embarrassed at his own insensitivity and arrogant presumptions that he knew how to make her feel good. "I'm so sorry. I never imagined you..." he wanted to make it sound better than sex, they had just had glorious moments together, "that you hadn't had sex before." Disbelief and anger at his own selfishness bombarded him.

"I'm sorry." Tears began flowing in earnest, and Keeva sat up.

Using a tissue, Tony took off the condom and threw it into a nearby wastebasket. She had moved to the edge of the bed and was sitting up. Her head flopped into her hands and he could see her shoulders shaking. He sat behind her, wrapping his legs around her and pulled her to his chest.

His stomach churned and he felt ill. He had hurt her and had been so selfish he didn't know her needs. "You don't need to apologize. I'm the barbarian that didn't even recognize the situation for what it was."

With her fingertips, she wiped the last tears from the corner of her eyes. He kissed the back of her head. Tony felt like the self-centered idiot he had been. Her first time, and he'd rammed into her like a jackhammer.

One of her wayward curls tickled Tony's nose and a nervous chuckle escaped him. He moved the mass of tangles to one side and kissed her now-bare shoulder.

Keeva was determined to try and hide the heat she had felt rise in her cheeks. She had been so naïve, making it worse by crying. She reached for a Kleenex from the nightstand. "Are you laughing at me, Salazar?"

"No, no, *chula*," he said. His voice was soft and sincere. "I would never laugh at you. You're so wonderful," He pulled her tighter against his chest.

Tony trickled his fingers down Keeva's side causing her muscles to flinch. "And you're ticklish." He brushed the back side of his hands down the other side.

Unable to control her sensitive skin, she flinched again. A smile she tried to suppress escaped. Goosebumps ran up her arms as Tony continued to run feathery tickles down her arms while kissing her neck. Any resistance or discomfort she had felt, melted at his tantalizing touch.

"Let me make it up to you. I don't want to leave it like this." Tony blew a soft breath on her neck and his fingers continued their torment on her stomach.

Without any doubts, she knew she had fallen for Tony. It was the reason she had decided to play the seduction card. Right now her life sat in turmoil but around Tony she felt on solid ground. She wanted to hold onto that, no matter what tomorrow brought. And no regrets, she would not have one more day with a regret.

The light tickling ignited scintillating tremors over her skin. His touch was delicate and slow but it felt like nirvana. "Look, Keeva." He moved one hand to point to their reflection in the antique mirror that topped her dresser.

He parted her legs with his hand. She had always avoided looking at herself naked, and not only was she seeing her most intimate anatomy but he was watching as well. The unfamiliar experience unchained some of her inhibitions and surprisingly, she liked it. Tony's eyes gleamed and his lips curved into a smile. She felt wicked and wonderful.

His fingers delved between her open thighs and went straight to her vaginal area. The few times she had ever had a man touch her so intimately, mirrors were not present. She closed her eyes in embarrassment.

"Open your eyes. You are perfection. Look at yourself." He moved her hair and kissed her neck. "I've never seen a woman so sensational." Tony's voice was husky and his hard erection at her back was proof his words were sincere.

He stroked her sensitive clitoris and her muscles pulsed in response. A desperate ache increased in her wet throbbing muscles. She had an overwhelming need to have him inside her. "I want you inside me, Tony. I need, I don't know, I need something."

"Mmm," Tony murmured in her ear, "I promise you'll be satisfied." He moved his hips against her back. "First, I want to please you."

Having him inside her would satisfy her, but she didn't want to ruin the moment. His stroke of her hypersensitive clit intensified the ache she felt. She watched as he slowly moved his fingers. He used his other hand to widen the folds, allowing them both a view of her most private area. It both embarrassed and enthralled her.

"How does this feel?" Tony's deep voice intoxicated her.

In the mirror, she could see her chest rising and falling. She wanted his hand on her nipples. "So good. I don't think I can stand it. I want your hands everywhere." She whispered. Trying to slow down the sensations that blitzed her, she calmed her breathing.

"Touch yourself, mi *amor*. Enjoy the pleasure, all of it."

Her eyes widened. She felt self-conscious, but wanted to obey his request. Tonight would be a night of memories, and she wanted to leave Tony with pleasurable memories as well. Besides, it felt naughty, yet thrilling at the same time.

"Here, here, let me show you." He moved her hands over her breasts. As her fingers touched her sensitive hard tips, she moaned.

"That's it." The mirror's reflection showed the desire in his eyes and she squirmed, pressing against him. He returned to stimulating her dewy folds and her muscles pulsed with excitement.

Keeva squeezed her aureoles between her thumbs and forefingers. She could see Tony's half-lidded eyes. She wanted to reach ecstasy and needed him inside her. "You're shameless. Your techniques for torture should get you arrested," she quipped. The growing onslaught was building to a crescendo.

"You are welcome to put me in handcuffs anytime." A low chuckle followed the comment.

A picture of him sprawled handcuffed to her bed piqued seductive ideas in her. These impulses were new and evocative, and she liked them.

Keeva could see her full breasts, the nipples peaked

and darker from her rubbing them. She laid her head back on Tony's shoulder, her mouth open, as she let out a sigh. "Don't stop. I can't take it." She put her hand on his, urging him to move faster.

"Slow, slow." He leaned back a little more, exposing a better view of her. "You're almost there. Relax."

Keeva felt like she would explode. His lips had moved into a half-smile. If this were a contest, he would no doubt win as the world's sexiest man. His broad shoulders filled the mirror, and the rippling muscles glistened with sweat.

Keeva rocked with the urgency. The heat of her clit spread through her and escalated with each stroke. Her breathing became erratic and bliss overtook her, sending her body into spasms. She sat upright, closing her legs on Tony's hands. He didn't move, his strong fingers holding her apart enough for him to continue stroking until the muscle contractions stopped. His half-smile became a grin.

She slumped back. "Do they teach you torture like that in the CIA?"

"You have no idea of the depths of my secret weapons." Tony moved aside and laid her down on the bed, following with his own body.

Keeva widened her legs, and Tony's erection slid comfortably between them.

"I don't want to hurt you. You're probably sore." He placed a gentle, healing kiss on her lips, and moved to her face and neck continuing the restorative gesture.

"I'm not sore. It felt a little tight but I'm fine. Embarrassed, feeling stupid and naïve, but not sore." Her voice was firm. "Please."

"Mmmm, you are remarkable." The kisses continued down her chest until he found the spot she had loved him nibbling. He bit the tip of her hard nipple.

Heat sizzled between her thighs joined by a scorching need. He put another condom on and resumed his position over her. His hard tip lay at her entrance and she spread her legs.

"You're driving me crazy." His voice was thick.

This time when he thrust inside her she opened for him. The flutter of longing, which had begun at the apex of her thighs, danced down her legs. "More, please," She begged. The out-of- control need had made her greedy. Her body ignited with a desire she couldn't describe.

He chuckled, rewarding her by thrusting deeper into her. Their rhythm strengthened. "How is that?" She couldn't answer.

Tony moved faster. Her skin felt like it was on fire as heat rose between them. "You are so responsive. *Dale*! I don't know how much longer I can hold out."

She let out a breath and moved with him. She thrust upward unable to control it any longer. "That's it. Yeah, enjoy it all."

Keeva dug her fingers into his back and raised her hips higher. Dropping her hands on the bed she grabbed a fistful of sheets and arched upward feeling Tony's powerful erection press against her muscles. Her orgasm was imminent. Elation and physical release spiraled through her, filling the desire that taunted her all night.

Tony continued his relentless movements and his breathing increased to gasps. He let out a loud groan and his body stiffened, and she felt the spasms of his release. After several more thrusts, he calmed and placed his head on her neck. She heard his frenzied breathing slow to an even pace. His spicy scent mixed with musk smoldered and she wished she could breathe him in forever.

He rolled off her and leaned up on one elbow. The dim light glimmered in lustful eyes. "That was astounding," he whispered and planted a quick kiss on her lips.

The constriction in Keeva's chest caused a gasp. She'd just had this one night of bliss. She doubted she'd ever experience this again. They lay languid in the bed, sleep threatening. "I want you to stay the night."

"I was hoping to, but before we fall asleep from exhaustion, let me go to my car and get the overnight bag."

*

He ignored the snow building up around him. The newspaper had described him with the hoodie, so he had switched to a ski cap and jacket. He could have used a warmer coat, but it didn't matter now. The burning anger raged in him.

He knew they had kept someone watching her after his screw up with the note. That had been a bad idea. It let them know he had access to her place and had ruined any chance he had of getting to her while she slept.

When he managed to turn it around by putting the note in the car crash victim's wallet, he'd hoped for a new chance. Now that asshole detective was in there with her. How could she? Their dark silhouettes came through the sheer curtains. He pulled his arms tighter to his sides and felt the skin break where his clenched fingers dug his nails into the skin.

Pain shot through his eye. He pushed his palm over it. This was all wrong. He began to feel the cold wet snow seeping through his sneakers. He stomped more and crossed his arms across his torso to block the cold wind.

Patience. He tried to follow all he had learned. He wanted to go over there and shoot both of them. They were lucky he didn't have his gun or he would have done just that.

He crouched down, the bitter cold turning his

fingers numb. The front door opened and Salazar sauntered out to his car. Relief and hope began to fill his bitter reserve. He crouched low, had to crawl behind the bushes to keep from being seen. It was dark but he didn't want to take any chances.

His muscles began shivering. He watched Salazar pull out a small duffle bag. "Damn it!" he said louder than he intended.

Salazar stopped walking and turned, looking around. He stopped moving, and for several long seconds remained perfectly still. Cold sweat dripped down his neck. His anger lessoned and his heartbeat increased. He held his breath trying to still himself. When the detective shrugged and walked in the door, he let out his breath.

A few minutes later, he gave up on watching Keeva and the jerk detective. He walked off and when he looked back, the swirling snow was covering his tracks. He smiled. It would work out; it always did.

*

An incessant noise rang and Keeva turned over, pulling the pillow over her head in an attempt to silence it. She smacked into something hard. Her eyes flew open. Tony's large brown chest with little brown curls blocked her view.

Lifting her gaze she saw he was clean shaven and he smelled like soap. He gave her a warm sweet smile and his brown eyes twinkled. The memories of the night before flooded her and she felt a renewed surge of heat. The sound stopped.

"*Buenas dias, querida.*"

"Is that a phone?" she groaned in a rough gravelly voice. The noise began again and she realized the buzzing was her own cell phone.

She swung around, reaching for her phone. "How the hell can you be so cheerful?" she snarled at him "And what time is it?" The ringing stopped.

"It's five." Tony lifted her chin.

Keeva tried not to think what her hair looked like. And her breath. *Oh, my God, I have morning breath. Maybe he does, too.* She doubted it. He looked like he had been up for some time.

She pushed herself up, but backed up so her breath didn't assault him. Keeva found her phone on the nightstand and pushed the awake button. She could see Lucy's number. Lucy had promised she'd open for her this morning. Maybe she'd forgotten her key.

She leaned back, and her head landed on his hard chest. "It's Lucy," she said as she held the phone up for him to see. "I hope she didn't forget her key."

"She could be locked out freezing to death in eight inches of snow."

"She just called, so she couldn't have been out too long."

He shook his head and grinned. "Nope. That is the third time she called."

Keeva bolted up. "What? Why didn't you wake me?" She never overslept. Except last night she and Tony had stayed up most of the night. Heat flushed her face as she remembered everything they'd done.

"You looked so peaceful, I just figured if it was important they'd keep calling back." He had leaned back into the headboard and pulled her back down so that her head rested on his chest. "Besides, I was selfish and wanted to watch you sleep."

Tipping her head back, she couldn't help but grin. She put her finger on the phone to press the call back number and his large hand went over hers. "I need to tell you something, Keeva." His voice was serious.

Keeva's phone rang and the sound startled her. She pushed the answer button but had noticed Tony's chest rise as though he had taken in a deep breath. He pulled his hand back and turned from her. "Keeva, I'm so sorry. It's a mess. The whole place. I'm so sorry. I don't know who did this. The police officer says..." Lucy's voice raised in pitch.

"The police? What? Calm down. You aren't making sense." Keeva moved to the edge of the bed, pulling the blanket with her. The mirror that had given her so much pleasure last night now reminded her what she looked like. She slid out of its view. Lucy never panicked, and hearing her so hysterical caused Keeva's throat to tighten.

"Someone broke in. I don't know what happened. Or even how long, since nothing was ready."

Keeva stood, wrapping the blanket around her. "What do you mean nothing was ready? Where is Tighe? Let me talk to him." Anger replaced Keeva's worry and she began pacing.

"He isn't here. The door was unlocked when I got here so I thought he might still be working. I looked all over and he wasn't here."

Keeva's knees felt like jelly. She knew that meant very little business today. She'd also let her customers down. Maybe she could get in and get some afternoon orders filled. But all her morning customers would be disappointed. That was something she couldn't afford. "I'm guessing you tried to call him."

"It was the first thing I did. I was going to start getting things ready, I figured we could still sell coffee and have lunch. Maybe get pastries and bread out later." There was an uncomfortable silence.

"I sense something stopped you." A throb began building in Keeva's head. Tony stood in front of her. His hair was damp, and he had on a pair of briefs. He looked like Adonis. She shrugged, the muscles across her upper back felt tight when she moved. What had she done to her back? The memory of an extended kiss that caused them both to fall over the couch answered her question.

Tony looked at her intently. She held up a finger letting him know it would be a minute.

"I'm sorry, Keeva. But someone tried to break open the safe." Keeva replayed the words in her mind. The room suddenly began turning on its edges. Her knees felt like they were giving out and the room began to darken. She leaned into the wall just as they stopped supporting her. Tony dropped down next to her and lifted her, setting her on the bed. He pulled the phone from her hand. A buzzing sound filled her head as he gently pushed her head to her knees. Air, she needed air.

In the distance she heard Tony's deep and calm voice. "Breathe deep. That's it, slow." She did her best to cooperate.

*

"I heard you on the phone earlier. Did you find out anything new about what happened?" Keeva asked Tony on the drive to the café.

He glanced sideways at her. "I called a friend at the FBI, and he's going to call me back." Tony reached over and placed a hand on her knee. "It's okay, you'll get through this."

His reassuring voice didn't remove the fear that still gnawed at her insides.

An officer met them at the door and called Tony aside. Keeva found Lucy in the dining room writing on a cardboard sign: Closed Today. Acid ate at Keeva's throat. This could mean the end of the café.

"Oh, Keeva." Lucy hugged her. "I'm sorry. I don't know what's going on. The police think Tighe did it. The door was open and he had a key, plus it looks like Tighe left town. They sent someone over to his apartment and it's empty."

Keeva knew Tighe had a criminal history, but believed it was a more petty crime. Why would he break into her storage closet? "They'll find him." She remembered the safe and on occasion they put off the bank deposit to the next day. Nausea roiled in her stomach. "What about the safe? Is anything missing?"

"It looks like someone tried to pry it open. They even broke the desk pushing it away. I think they wanted to take the whole safe but couldn't get it out."

Keeva was thankful she had had the safe screwed down. It had been a suggestion from the builder who'd remodeled. He had told her he'd had a client who'd had a safe carried away. She sent up a mental prayer of thanks.

"There wasn't much cash in the safe. I deposited last night's cash, so the only money they took was the petty cash."

That still left the company's credit cards and important documents, including her grandmother's handwritten recipes. Only she, Lucy and Mac had access to the safe. The petty cash was kept in a locked drawer but most of the employees knew where they kept the key. It was only a hundred dollars in small bills.

"Is that all they took?" She felt like *Alice In Wonderland* stepping into the rabbit hole. Nothing made sense. If she'd had a business that kept something worth taking she would comprehend this happening. Why would someone break into a café?

"No. That's what is so odd." Lucy looked perplexed and shook her head.

Keeva needed to sit. Fatigue and stress had zapped her energy and she was having trouble focusing on Lucy's words. She had wanted to prove she could make it, that she was more than the lost and lazy person her parents had believed her to be. So far she was failing miserably. "What else is missing?" Keeva arched her back, trying to stretch out the tightness she felt.

Lucy slanted her head and furrowed her brows. To Keeva it looked like something mystified her. But what wasn't perplexing about someone trying to rob a café with very little cash. "The closet you locked downstairs. The lock was broken off and most of the stuff in it is missing or dumped." Tears filled Lucy's large blue eyes. "I'm sorry, Keeva."

Keeva placed her elbows on her thighs, intertwined her fingers, and looked up at Lucy. "It's not your fault. I'm glad whoever did this left before you got here. I could not bear you getting hurt."

Tony stood at the door speaking on his cell phone. Keeva couldn't make out what he said, until he spoke, "What?!" loud enough for everyone to hear. The tightness in his pinched lips confirmed what she heard in his voice. He was angry. He turned and moved back into the kitchen and she could no longer hear him. Bewildered by his sudden outburst, she stepped toward the kitchen when Lucy's hand stopped her.

Lucy's tear streaked face brightened. She leaned closer to Keeva and whispered, "I forgot about last night. How did it go?"

So intent on Tony's anger, Lucy's words took a second to register. The memory of last night and all the new experiences sent heat up Keeva's neck. She cleared her throat, "Um, fine." The words squeaked out.

Lucy squealed and jumped, clapping her hands. "He stayed over?" Lucy looked cautiously back at the way Tony had gone. "That's why you guys came over together." Keeva nodded.

Tony had wandered back to the doorway, the phone still at his ear. He appeared less angry and more worried. He was dialing again. She wondered what could be going on.

"The night went well." Keeva didn't plan on sharing the details with Lucy, so she didn't say anymore. She pointed to the front door, "Put the sign out. Write it was due to a break in. Maybe someone saw something." Keeva walked over to Tony as he ended the call.

Tony sauntered over to her as he placed the phone in his pocket. His lips turned up into a small, reassuring smile.

Lack of sleep came over Keeva and she yawned. The world around her fell apart and she wanted to ignore it all and go to bed. Tony put his arms around her back and pulled her into his chest. The overt sign of affection surprised Keeva. She looked up at him.

"Tired?" His voice was a low growl that sounded as sexy as he looked. She wondered if he ever looked bad.

Yesterday the case ended, and she presumed their relationship would, too. No regrets, she told herself. Now she had none, or did she? Tony had been the bright spot in her life lately. His constant support helped her through all the bizarre happenings. Yes, Tony liked her. She doubted he would lie. But she had fallen in love with him, the indescribable sensation she felt in her chest when he looked at her coupled with the steady rhythm of all her senses when he stood near her, supported that.

Keeva's silent promise to her parents had been what kept her going before. She needed to focus on the business. After this morning, she doubted Tony'd stick around. Since he met her there had been nothing but chaos around her. The emotional roller coaster of worrying if he'd stick around, would leave her feelings in a tumultuous mess. No, she had to focus on the business and put aside any thoughts of a serious relationship with Tony. It hurt to think about it, but last night had left her with good memories. Walking away would never be easy so the quicker it ended the easier it would be for her.

"What did you find out?"

"There were no signs of a forced entry. Someone let himself in with a key. It all points to Tighe." Tony said.

None of this made sense to Keeva. "Why would Tighe do this?" Keeva pulled out the stool under the counter and sat.

"According to my FBI contact, Tighe has a history of some pretty sordid behavior."

Keeva sighed. She wanted this whole day over. Weariness, a deep down in her bones type, had settled over her. A lump rose in her throat but she did not want to begin crying again. Not this time. She swallowed back impending tears with the pressure in her throat. "What did you find out?"

"Nothing good." He shook his head and Keeva noticed the lines in his face had deepened. Maybe all her issues were beginning to wear him out as well.

"He comes from the Seattle area. His family owned a bakery and he worked there when he was a kid." Tony stopped to look at his buzzing phone. "It's a detective from Seattle. I have to take this." Keeva listened to Tony's end of the conversation with antici-pation, but he didn't say much, he mostly listened.

Tony stepped back in front of Keeva, opened his mouth to speak, closed it and shook his head. Keeva could almost feel his irritation when he hardened his jaw before he spoke. "The more I find out about the man, the angrier I get that he's not in prison." His voice was tense. "Our boy Tighe likes to gamble, too. He pretty much ran the family business into the ground. In 1990 he was charged with racketeer-ing. It was mostly local gambling, done through the phone and with runners, and if someone brought in more people they upped the percent of their winnings. Tighe was the gambling version of Salesman-of-the-Year. The police suspect he used any means possible, beatings, blackmail, extortion, you name it to force people to gamble."

"Did he go to prison?"

"Eventually. Spent two years locked up. That last call was one of the detectives who helped convict him and he said Tighe came out of prison a changed man. Unfortunately, he changed for the worse, not the bet-ter. Within months of his release, his ex-wife charged him with assault, his parents fired him and had to get a restraining order on him."

Tony pulled up another stool and sat facing Keeva. Those brown eyes of his hit her right in her gut. She could stare at them all day. "There's more. You sure you want to hear this?" He grabbed her hands and held them.

"Yes, I do." Her voice sounded hollow. She would rather not hear it but she knew she needed to.

"A year after he was released his parents were found murdered and no one has ever been charged with the crime. This detective believes it was a professional hit. Though he has no proof, he says he'd swear Tighe hired the killer. He had a rock solid alibi, but he was the sole heir to a hefty life insurance policy."

Tony's words hammered at Keeva. She had done a background check and hadn't learned any of this. She opened her mouth to speak, but Tony stopped her with his finger over her lips.

Tony placed his hands on her shoulders. "Don't blame yourself. It took me weeks to find this information." He was giving her the bad news gently. "My FBI friend said even they didn't have this guy high on their radar. Not as Tighe Arthur anyway." Tony waited for her response but she didn't trust herself to speak and just nodded.

"He isn't Tighe Arthur. His real name is Tighe Kaykerten. Tighe Arthur is his *latest* alias. He left extortion and robbery charges behind in Idaho under the name Tighe Kay and John Kay. In Idaho, he worked for a mom and pop baker where he ordered large amounts of bakery equipment and charged it to the business. The owners found out when he opened a nearby establishment. It took him two years to do it, but he used their money."

The whole thing sounded preposterous and Keeva laughed. "I'm sorry, I know this isn't funny. But at least he is a baker. I made one right decision in hiring him."

Tony's eyes softened and his sweet half-smile returned for a second. "We think the baking kept him looking legit. They suspect he kept up the gambling by starting his own business. He upped the ante. Instead of hiring runners to place bets and deliver winnings, the customers had to come into the shop. By eliminating the runners, he saved thousands of dollars a week. This way he kept more of the profit."

"God, I can't believe I didn't suspect anything."

"Not your fault. Nobody knew who he was. The FBI only looked into it because I called."

After a pause, he continued. "All the small players they caught testified they were coerced by Tighe or one of his men to get involved and bring in more customers. One person said they'd rather face gambling charges than deal with another beating." Tony shook his head. Keeva knew Tony had little tolerance for violence.

Keeva stood and walked to the coffee machine and poured a cup for her and one for Tony. He placed his hand over hers when she held out the cup. Those fingers had touched her most intimate parts and brought her to ecstatic heights.

"It looks like he tried to do the same to you. You had said someone was ordering large amounts of supplies and equipment. But since you were on top of it, I'd guess he had more trouble than he planned. What did you have in the closet downstairs?"

Keeva closed her eyes, making a mental list of the unordered supplies. "I sent the last mixer back yesterday. There was a scale and some smaller equipment. Most of it has been picked up and sent back."

"Let's go look. Gary should be done processing down there and you'll have to turn in a list of what's missing."

Before stepping off the stairs, Keeva could smell the sweet sauces she kept locked up. She stopped at the end of the stairs, the door to the storage area was open a few inches but splintered wood stuck out from the lock. From here it didn't look too disastrous, the vanilla and chocolate sauce leaked under the door, blending like swirled ice cream.

Behind her, she could hear Tony breathing. His cell phone buzzed in his pocket but he didn't answer it. Mac was on the way over, but she wanted Tony with her as she dealt with all this. Something about the way he always stood near her, noticed her little reactions and reassured her she could do this.

Stepping around the viscous sauces, she pulled

open the door and froze. "Damn it." She closed her eyes and wished it would all go away. The feeling of someone invading her space, just like finding the note in her apartment, sucked out any sense of security she had left. "Why? Why is someone doing this to me?" This time she didn't care if Tony saw her cry and she let her tears flow. The undulation of her emotions left her unsteady and weak.

The storage area had shelves on all the walls surrounding a refrigerator. In the center of the room sat a butcher-block work bench. The flours, sugars and cocoa powder blended into the jars of fruit preserves covering the floor. Broken glass and boxes protruded from the mess. It looked like bad modern art.

Keeva bent and began numbly picking up glass. Tony, who had not said a word, leaned over her and pulled her up by her elbows. "Don't worry about that. Let's call a cleaning company to come in."

"No, no. I'm tired of being the victim. I am not going to let this creep do this to me. I will fix it." It dawned on Keeva that whoever did this, could have been stalking her. "Do you think Tighe is the one who stalked me? Could he have wanted to frighten me?" As tiny drops of water would fill a bucket, little bits of her helplessness changed to anger.

"No. I don't think they are related. Tighe is a thug and you would have recognized him the night he came out of the bushes. Unless he hired someone to get into your apartment, I don't think breaking and entering is something he could have pulled off so easily."

Tony pulled her to him and wrapped his arms around her. She leaned her head on his chest. He felt so solid and smelled so good. She inhaled his musky scent. His arms wrapped around her made her feel comfortable and safe. If only they could remain like this all day. "I think Tighe lashed out because you got in his way, your diligence kept him from opening another location." His voice rumbled in his chest, and she felt his cell phone on his hip buzz again.

"Take your calls, Tony. I know you have to work." She stepped away from his warmth.

He pulled the phone out and looked at it. "It's my FBI contact." He hit the button and said, "Hang on a sec." He looked at Keeva and said, "Make sure Gary is finished before you touch anything." Tony turned back to the phone, "Salazar here," he continued and stepped out of the storage room.

The crime scene tech had been packing up his tackle box and putting away his camera. A female officer who looked familiar stood talking to him. How many cops had she talked to in the last few weeks? By now she'd probably met most of the police force, she told herself sarcastically.

Gary worked quickly and the officer asked some of the same questions she had been repeating too often lately. After the technician left, Lisbeth, the officer, stopped writing. "Keeva, I know this is hard, there has been a lot of crap going on. If you need anything, if I can help, let me know, okay?" She made eye contact with Keeva as though expecting a response. Keeva kept quiet. "Tony is a big support, but there are others in the department concerned for you as well. So don't go through this alone."

"Thanks." Keeva wanted to say more. She felt grateful for all their help and support, but right now she couldn't find the words. Lisbeth handed Keeva her card and stopped to talk to Tony before she left.

Keeva had to step through the syrupy mess to get to garbage bags. The goo crawled up her leather boots and she was sure they would ruin. "Son of a bitch," she mumbled as she pulled her foot out of more of the sticky mess. "I'll strangle Tighe myself if I ever see him."

She heard Mac holler down the stairs. He grabbed the frame of the door and stopped himself from propelling into the slime. "Holy shit!" He looked around at the mess and then at Keeva.

Lucy poked her head out behind Mac. Without saying a word, Lucy stepped around Mac with a shovel and a bucket in her hand.

"I'll start getting the mess off the floor." She turned to Mac, "Could you help me? This way Keeva can move around and see what is missing."

Keeva was grateful for Lucy's assertiveness. Mac still held the door frame.

"Mac, here." He blinked as though seeing Lucy for the first time. He grabbed Lucy's outstretched shovel and stepped into the mess, walking over to Keeva.

Hugging her with the free arm, he said, "I'm sorry. I don't know what I can do, but I'll stay here with you until we get this all straightened out."

The support was what she needed. The mess around her didn't feel quite so overwhelming anymore.

Tony came back to the door. "Can you come here a sec, Keeva?"

She followed him out of the storage area. He looked concerned and she crossed her arms, steeling herself for more bad news.

"They got Tighe." No emotion, no cheers, he sounded flat.

Confused by his bland reaction, she wondered if he was just being a cop and separating himself from last night.

"That's good news, isn't it?"

"Yes, it is good news. The BOLO alert worked. Someone spotted his car crossing from Montana into Idaho. Since he has warrants there and Washington, I'm not sure we'll get him back here." He held her shoulders and fixed his gaze on her. "Charges will be pressed. My concern is we might not be able to extradite him here. They are going to look back at his parent's death." He sounded more like her attorney, announcing the news to her, than the spellbinding man who had taken her virginity the night before.

She pulled back. The whole mess, the whole fear of a stalker, of losing her business, none of it gave her the anguish that twisted through her right now. Bitterness burned in her throat. Maybe before all this she could have imagined something between her and Tony, but now it all hung in doubt. Business had just begun to pick up, but this was all a setback. And she had promised her parents, herself, hell, even Mac and Betty. They all had some money invested in the café. She owed it to them, she owed it to herself to make it work. "I guess I never thought of that. But they got him." Her voice was raspy.

Tony put his hands in his pockets and dropped his head. "I have to go to the office and file a report. There's other work, so I'm not sure when…"

Keeva put up her hand and interrupted him, "It's okay, Tony. Go, go to work. I'm fine here. They have Tighe, they have the stalker, now you need to get the attacker. I get it." She turned and walked to the storage room before he could see the renewed bout of tears she held back.

Right now she had to tackle this mess, but soon she had to come to terms with being in love with a man who might not feel the same, who might be all-work, who might not have time for or interest in a relationship. This tipped the scale in the wrong direction. "Wait." She called back to Tony. When he turned to look at her, his head tilted.

Keeva needed to sort things out, first with the mess here, and then the business. After she sorted them, she could deal with her heart. She owed her parents that much, to be serious about her future. "I'm…" she closed her eyes and swallowed down the lump that built in her throat. "I'm not sure about, well, about a few things right now." Tony searched her face, his eyes darkened. She suspected they hid his own emotions. Emotions he had never told her. Yes, her decision would be better, she reassured herself. "I need time, Tony. I need to concentrate on the business. I promised myself after my parent's died…." She paused again, forcing herself to say the words. "I hope you understand."

Tony didn't say a word, he turned and left.

Pausing away from where Mac and Lucy could see her, she heard Tony walk up the stairs. Her knees buckled and she sank against the wall and sobbed. A few minutes later she felt Lucy's arms wrap around her. "It's okay. Mac and I will help. You'll get through this." Like a dam released, her tears freely flowed and she sobbed into Lucy's comforting arms.

Tony ascended the stairs with as much enthusiasm as walking to death row. Leaving Keeva had been difficult, but she wanted it. He saw the pain in her face and knew he had put it there. He had failed her, failed to protect her. Last night he'd given her pleasure, but he'd been unable to bring her happiness. She made that clear.

When they had lain in bed that morning, he had planned on telling Keeva how he felt. Lucy's phone call interrupted him before he could. Now he knew it was better. She had made it clear. All his relationships ended because he'd been unable to communicate clearly and to commit.

He chuckled a bitter laugh. How ironic, this time the woman he fell for, the woman he wanted to spend the rest of his life with, didn't love him.

He'd walked to his car and barely registered the bright sun and warming temperatures. Opening the car, he turned and looked back at the café. Several people milled about in front, and a small group, huddled and chatting, walked away from the porch, the sign out front had notified them of the café's closing.

A temptation to walk back in and ask her if there was any chance their relationship might work passed as quick as it came. Closing the car door, he could still smell her scent lingering. He missed her already.

Maybe she didn't care for him, maybe he would have to live with the love he felt for her. But still, he could find the attacker. Keeva had saved Todd and Madison's lives and the best thing he could do was find the monster that hurt those teens.

*

Keeva drank the last of the coffee. Mac and Lucy came upstairs. "The storage room is finished." Lucy said putting away the mop.

"Thanks. I faxed the inventory to the police."

Mac came and stood by her. "You look exhausted, sis. I'll drive you home."

She remembered she had come in with Tony and didn't have her car. "I'm not going to argue." She stood, grabbed her purse and turned to Lucy, "Are you sure you're okay opening up for a little while?"

"Yes, let me do that. I cannot understand why you won't let me come in tonight. I can get a nap and come in after midnight." Lucy looked at her with those large doe eyes and sounded disappointed.

"I need you and Mac to help out during the day. You know the business side and Mac is great with the customers." She sighed. She hated not being there to help Lucy salvage what little they could for the day. Lucy and Mac had been insistent they at least open up for lunch and the afternoon crowd. They had some baked goods in the freezer that hadn't been touched and there was always the fancy coffees so many people loved.

She felt grateful for all the calls of support that had come across her phone. Her customers, even competing businesses offered help. It was hard enough to be in debt with the bank and she wouldn't put herself in that spot with loyal customers and friends, so she told everyone they were fine.

The sunshine and big blue sky did little to warm her when they walked to the car. Mac had been sweet enough to keep quiet about her meltdown. She figured he and Lucy thought it was the damage in the café that caused it. Maybe that had contributed, but only she knew the stress was about the events combined with the situation with Tony.

"Where's your car?" Mac asked when they pulled up in front of her house a few hours later.

"I put it in the garage before the snow came last night. Otherwise the plow piles snow around it." She was thankful the day had turned warm and that the snow had melted. Maybe she would run to work tomorrow.

"Are you sure you don't want me to come in tonight? I don't sleep much anyway."

Keeva wanted to hug her brother, but feared if she did she'd begin bawling all over again. "No, Mac. There is no need to. I'm safe, remember? The stalker is dead and they have Tighe. I need you and Lucy to run the café." She grabbed the door handle but wanted to give Mac a little more reassurance. "Neither of you know the baking end. I did it all in the beginning. I really need you to work with Lucy, it's going to take a few weeks for her get the whole grasp of running the business end. If you manage the kitchen and up front, she can focus on that." She opened the door and stepped out of the car. Leaning back in, she asked, "That would be the best help I can get. Then I can relax and focus on the baking until I can find a replacement." She waved and shut the door.

CHAPTER 9

FIVE STEPS LEFT, five spaces right, five spaces left...He counted each step before turning. When his father, Lars Smith had been alive, he had begun each teenager's training with all-night lookouts. Two boys would spend the night pacing at the road, five steps left and five steps right. They covered a multitude of training exercises if they did what Lars had told them. The marching kept them awake, but seven hours of marching in all types of weather had increased their stamina. All the young men who trained under his father had become excellent hunters, able to track an animal for as long as had been necessary. It had also been an honor and privilege, the first step before they became one of the men and could join the meetings.

A few families left the militia because they believed

his father treated the boys too harshly. But he never complained, he endured, and had become a better man for it.

As the son of The Free Militia's founder and leader, he had moved up quicker than the other teenagers. By fourteen, they'd accepted him as a full member. He had paid his dues, though. As people left the organization, Lars became increasingly bitter. Some days he took it out on his mother, but most days he took it out on him.

Straightening his shoulders, he continued the pace. After an hour of pacing, he knew what he would do next.

He'd taken his vacation from work and had planned on having Keeva with him tonight. The idiots around her had her confused. His duty would be to convince her she belonged to him. Another act of endurance he had prepared for.

He drove to Capital City and pulled up to the café. Seeing a handmade sign and the front door closed surprised him, but not as much as seeing a police cruiser parked in the driveway. He saw Jimmy. Raw rage filled him. He detested seeing him and contemplated leaving but tossed aside the idea with a better plan. He'd use Jimmy to get more information since Jimmy was a cop.

Stepping from his car, he approached the despicable man's police cruiser and leaned on the driver's side.

"Hey, Dillon," said Jimmy as he opened the window.

"Hey, watz up?" He delivered the line with a plastered-on smile. He'd rather eat shit than be nice to him, but it was all part of the plan.

"Just keeping watch on the café."

"Why? What happened?"

"An employee did some damage and broke a few things." He sensed Jimmy had guarded his words.

"Are they closed for good?"

"No, they opened for a few hours this afternoon. I'm just here to make sure nothing else happens."

"Is anyone else here?" He wanted to know if Keeva was inside.

"Nope. Just me."

"I mean inside. I can see there's no one out here."

Like a bad actor in a cheap spaghetti western, Jimmy pushed his aviator sunglasses down his nose. "Does it look like anyone is in there, Dillon? Like I said, they only opened for a few hours. Go over to Delicious Donuts for your pastry fix." Jimmy pushed the obnoxious glasses back in place.

He wanted to shove the glasses down Jimmy's throat, but instead he tapped the frame of the car door and said, "Yeah, I just might."

He turned and went back to his car. He didn't feel like dealing with Jimmy today. Whoever had done this had torpedoed his plans. A gnawing began at the back of his chest. Keeva always stayed after closing, and he wondered why tonight was different. It was late in the day and he had planned to bring Keeva back to the cabin tonight.

Pulling the car from the curb, it took all his control to not give Jimmy the finger. The asshole lifted his hand in half a wave. He rolled his eyes.

He drove past Keeva's house. The windows looked dark. He pulled his car in front of another car several houses away. Able to watch her apartment through his side view mirror, he did so with his jaw clenched. It was the only sign of his growing impatience. He smiled and congratulated himself at his ability to hide his emotions.

The memory of the detective at her apartment had seared in his mind and it ate at him. Maybe Keeva had gone to the detective's place. The muscle under one eye began twitching. He rubbed it to no avail, the annoying tic continued.

"Damn it." Infuriated at himself for not finding the detective's address, he made the decision to drive through the neighborhoods. Finding one of two cars in Capital City couldn't be that hard.

Two hours later, he still hadn't found the address or seen Keeva. The snow had melted, but the warm Chinook winds had stopped blowing and another cold front settled over the Capital City Valley. Dillon parked the car at the end of a dead end street that backed up to a city park.

He exited the car. The inability to locate Keeva increased his frustration. He needed to pace. Initially, he kept the cadence slow and even but each time he thought about Keeva, and worried she could be with Salazar, he lost his pace. He counted aloud trying to concentrate, "One, two, three," but lost count. He did an about-face, "One, two, three, four…" His hands balled, and he pounded them down toward the ground, "Damn," he hollered at the dirt. He had just gone that way. Maybe not, but he had done five paces which meant he needed to start over. Violent, painful, flashes pulsed behind his eye.

"Stupid, stupid," the cold air amplified his words but he no longer cared if anyone heard him. The last time he had pain this severe, he had run into those two idiots, Madison and Todd. When he tried to talk to Todd, Todd had ignored him. He had made him pay.

Part of his job had been to be at the local high school football games and he'd met several of the players, including Todd. Another time he saw him leaving a game with Madison and introduced himself to Madison and she drew back when he offered his hand. Todd and his friends had laughed. The humiliation he'd felt soon turned to a vow for revenge.

A few weeks later as he walked around downtown

late at night, he ran into Todd. He stopped Todd and wanted to make him apologize, but Todd called him a weirdo and walked away. Curious why Todd had been in that part of town he'd began following him and Madison. He soon discovered their rendezvous up by the Fire Tower and followed their route to Madison's house. When he discovered they routinely went through the alley, he'd formulated his plan. He managed to hurt Todd and would have done the same to Madison, but Keeva had stepped in.

Madison was nothing next to Keeva. He understood Keeva was the one for him. His mother always took the pain away, but he didn't have her anymore. She knew how to soothe him, sometimes he didn't like where she touched him, but it made him feel better. Somehow, she had managed to make it all better. The doctors had prescribed drugs but they made him sleep. He'd become aware of the cure by accident. He had hit a deer on a side street and he had watched it die. The pain in his head drained as he watched the deer's life bleed away. And afterward he had felt alive.

Someone yelled from a distance. He stopped moving. A car door slammed in the same area. He heard a male voice yell. "Get back here, bitch!" Could it be a lover's quarrel?

He hurried to his car and drove to the end of the short street, parking so a row of hedges hid the car from the crossing street. Scrambling out of the car, he crouched low, staying behind the hedges. Pushing the thorny branches aside, He could see a female walking in his direction and the tail lights of a car as it screeched away.

The female looked thin and not too tall, but her steps were quick. He watched as she wiped her eyes. Maybe the night wasn't such a waste after all. The pain in his head began to ease. He figured she wouldn't expect him to be there, which made her an easy target. She was about four houses away. He had to act fast.

He had left the engine running in his car. He stepped back to the car and popped the trunk, grabbing the syringe of Versed. He watched through the bushes. She was one house away. He could hear her sniffle and mumble to herself. He let her walk by him before he stepped out. He covered her mouth before she could yell and pushed the syringe toward her. The medication would take a few minutes to take affect so he needed to get her in the trunk as soon as he injected it.

She looked young, maybe sixteen or seventeen. Her eyes opened wide and filled with fright as she twisted around and looked at his face. Squirming, she managed to loosen her arms and began pulling down on his hand. Trying to stop her squirming, he used both hands to wrap around her and dropped the syringe.

He pulled her toward the car. If he could get her

in the trunk, he could drive away and stop later to get the Versed into her. She tripped over something and began to topple to the ground. Her forward momentum pulled his hand loose and she began to scream. He grabbed her mouth. He had to shut the bitch up. She bit down on his hand. "Fuck!" He let go and she fell to the ground. Despite his gloves, it still felt like she pierced his skin.

That's when it all went to hell. She scrambled on all fours into the street and began shrieking like a banshee. The rapid fire pounding in his chest caused pressure that shot to his brain. The air around him became thick and he had trouble breathing. Reaching for her again, he felt like he would fall. Her wailing became louder.

He heard a dog bark. "What's going on here?" someone shouted.

He looked up. A man, holding a large dog on a leash, ran in his direction. Shit, he had to get out of here. Damn it, he was so close but the girl had stood and had begun running toward the man.

He jumped into the car, and the man lunged at the door, grabbing the door's handle. He hit the gas pedal. The man fell when he swerved the car and he saw the man tumble to the asphalt. He drove down the street, lights still out, and turned on more streets, unsure where he was going. A few blocks away he pulled over and shut the trunk.

"Damn it!" He stomped on the ground and felt an exploding pain in his head. He grabbed his head with both hands and flopped back into the front seat of the car.

*

Tony arrived on the scene and stepped out from his car. He sighed. A scene of pandemonium was sprawled before him. Why did it always look so chaotic? Chaos irritated him. He wanted someone in charge and keeping things calm, a rarity in police work. Neighbors outside, police cars, police with flashlights, an ambulance driving away, lights swirling, and more people than he cared to count. His eyes scanned the area looking for anyone in uniform before spying Officer Jimmy Smith. His eyes closed and he drew in a deep breath. The gods were not on his side tonight.

"Hi, Jimmy. Looks like a carnival out here. What's going on?" Tony asked, feeling like his effort to sound civil had become lost in the chatter of bystanders.

"We got a call about an attempted abduction, young girl, sixteen, Kimberly Jones, walking home after drinking with some friends." He pointed his flashlight from where they stood toward a main road. "A Mr. Jameson was walking his dog and heard her scream. A few other neighbors said they heard the kids yelling from a car parked down the street. They heard the door slam and the car screech away." Jimmy aimed the flashlight from where the neighbors heard the kids closer to them. He then shone it right behind them, on the intersection of the street. "Best we can figure out someone waited for her here and grabbed her."

"Who called it in?" Tony had a bad feeling about all this. Something at the back of his brain told him he was missing something. He couldn't place it.

Jimmy looked at his notepad. "The dog walker, Mr. Jameson." Jimmy shone his flashlight in the direction of a man sitting on the curb. A paramedic was applying a sling to his arm.

Tony sighed and swore to himself that TJ would be in every night by sundown until he went to college. "What about the people who heard the kids yelling? And where is the guy who dumped her and drove away?"

Jimmy looked over at the girl and shook his head. "A patrol car went to his house. She claims he's her boyfriend, the boyfriend says he isn't. Idiots." Jimmy looked at Tony and shrugged. "He lives with a roommate, and the roommate swears he was home at five past eleven. That conflicts with being here five minutes later." Jimmy turned to talk to one of the other police officers, then went back to Tony. "They've brought him into the station."

"Any thoughts on this?" Tony was surprised at Jimmy's cooperation. It was so different from past cases.

Jimmy looked over at the girl. "It's probably not

the boyfriend, but we're going to keep him until we know he wasn't involved. She claims she'd never seen the guy who attacked her before." Tony rubbed his forehead with the back of his hand still unable to place what was wrong. "Where is she now?"

"She's in the ambulance." Jimmy pointed toward the vehicle whose bright lights danced in the night sky. "But there is something else," he paused. "We found a syringe."

Tony felt the blood drain from his own face and he felt a hollow fear filled his gut.

"Gary collected it. The label read *Versed*," Jimmy said.

A violent chill ran through Tony's limbs. He tightened his jaw, clamping down his teeth. The attacker was back.

Jimmy stepped off the curb, and then turned back to Tony as though he had just remembered something, "The syringe top found at the first attack and now this, I don't believe in coincidences, do you?" Jimmy turned and walked away, the words trailed behind him.

The dreaded realization that the attacker had struck again hit Tony like a slug to his chest. He never completely accepted the notion that the stalker and attacker were two different people. Granted, they still could be, but he didn't want to take any chances. With his hand, he motioned to Jimmy to wait. He dialed Keeva's number. She didn't answer.

She'd made it clear she didn't want a relationship and the distance in her emotions had cut him like a knife. Her life has been hell the last few weeks, and she deserved to display any outbursts. Around Keeva he found his emotional compass, he felt grounded. At the same time, he knew she needed a man who could return the same. Not walk away like he did.

He dialed again. No answer.

Tony wondered if she was ignoring him. Maybe she was asleep. He smiled at the memory of her sleeping so soundly buried deep under the comforter this morning.

When she didn't answer after the third try, warning signals shot through him like a Taser. He looked at his watch, it was nearly midnight, but Mack kept weird hours, so he decided to call him so he could warn Keeva to be careful.

"Hey, Salazar, what is it with you and the late hours?" Mac laughed into the phone. Tony liked the guy. They had kept in touch over the last few weeks, and he found Mac to be as sincere as Keeva, though less driven.

"It's a perk they give you with the job. You should join us. You could be having as much fun as I am."

"Don't tempt me. I've been toying with the idea. Anyway, what gives?"

"I can't get Keeva on her phone. It looks like there has been another attack and it might be the original attacker." Tony's throat tightened at the whole scenario. "And all night something about this has been familiar. I just want to make sure she's home and safe." He also wanted an excuse to talk to her, but kept that to himself.

There was a few seconds of silence before Mac spoke again. "Crap. She's working tonight."

"Working?" *Mierda.* Tony wanted to hit someone.

"Yeah. You know her. Lucy and I offered, but she said she felt safe with the stalker dead and Tighe in jail."

Tony couldn't push aside the bad feeling that had nagged at him all night. "Would you go over there and check on her. A teen girl was attacked and it's chaos around here, so I can't get away right now. I just want to know she's okay and let her know this guy is still out there."

"Fuck. I knew I should have never let her work alone. I'll go over now and give her a lecture for not answering her phone."

"You could try calling first. It might just be me she's ignoring."

"I doubt that one, bro. She's all teenage lovesick every time you're around." Mac laughed. "I won't sleep knowing this guy might be out there again. She works with her earplugs in and music on so that's probably why she isn't hearing the phone."

"All right. Just get to her, okay?"

"Getting in the car now. I'll be there in a couple of minutes."

"Thanks!" Knowing Mac was checking on Keeva relieved Tony's anxiety, a little.

When the second ambulance left the scene about ten minutes later, Tony moved back to his car and his cell phone rang. He read the screen. "What is it, Mac?"

"It's not good, Tony. Keeva's not at the café, but Henry is. He's been shot. Thankfully, he's conscious. Looks like a flesh wound. I called 9-1-1 and they're on the way."

Tony's legs felt like they were going to give out from under him. He grabbed his car door for support. For the first time in a very long time he felt real fear. "What do you mean she's not there? What does Henry say?"

"He doesn't know. He's pretty shaken up and rambling about the crazy man that's like a cat. It doesn't look too serious but he's losing blood so I'm trying to keep him calm until the ambulance comes."

The tightening of Tony's muscles were all that kept him standing. It felt like a huge hole had just opened in the ground and swallowed him up. Keeva was missing. Henry had described the stalker as a cat. Could the son of a bitch have taken her?

"I'll be right there!"

Tony's car radio started squawking and he could

see the other uniformed officers responding to theirs. Everyone started moving and it seemed like everything was happening in slow motion and he had trouble focusing on what to do next. He stepped up, moved over to Jimmy at the same time Jimmy finished responding to his radio.

"I'm heading to Keeva's. Mac's there, someone is shot, and Keeva hasn't been located."

Jimmy's eyes hardened. "I just got the call. I have to go to the hospital, but I'll be there as soon as I can."

Tony called into dispatch. He needed to get someone to help with the interviews, because he planned to find Keeva.

The ride to the café felt like the longest two minutes in Tony's life. He used all his expertise to block the scenarios that filtered into his imagination, scenarios that didn't turn out well for Keeva.

The ambulance lights cut through the night air and two patrol SUVs pulled up behind Tony. He was half out of the car as he threw the shift into park and pulled the key out of the ignition.

He reached the door at the same time the two medics arrived with their gear. Not wanting to wait, he began pushing past them when he felt a hand grab his upper arm. He whipped around to knock off the offender's hand. It was Lisbeth, the patrol officer.

"Easy, Tony, let them get in there." Her voice,

steady and calm, brought Tony back to the reality that Henry was hurt.

"I'm sorry, I need to see what is happening." The medics went through the door and Tony followed close behind.

Mac kneeled over a very pale Henry. A pool of blood ran down Henry's side. Mac held a cloth over the wound but stood and moved when the medics bent over Henry. As he approached Tony, blood covered his hands and he visibly shook.

"How is he? Is he saying anything about Keeva." Tony asked.

"He's okay. The bleeding has slowed down." Mac walked toward the sink and began washing the blood from his hands. "I think he's more traumatized about Keeva. Some guy held the gun to him and told him to knock on the door. He told him he'd kill Keeva if he didn't. Poor guy knocked to save her."

"Did he hurt Keeva?" Tony felt frantic.

"According to Henry, the guy pulled Keeva's arm and that's when Henry tried to stop him and got shot. He said it looked like he punched her with something and then dragged her out by the arm."

Mac splashed water over his face and turned toward Tony. "Shit. I can't believe this is happening." Mac shook his head and reached for a glass, filled it with water and took a long drink.

Scott, Tony's supervisor, walked through the

kitchen door. He stopped and spoke to the medics and then walked over to Mac and Tony. "What's going on?"

Scott gave Tony a bolster of hope. He had always been Tony's mentor and through his career in the Capital City P.D. Other than Mari, Scott was the only person who knew Tony's feelings toward Keeva.

Mac and Scott shook hands and introduced themselves. With a nod toward Mac, Tony encouraged him to continue. Mac repeated what he told Tony before adding, "Fuck it all. I didn't want her to work alone. I wish I hadn't listened to her." His voice was hoarse.

Tony's throat tightened at the strangling in Mac's voice. He worried Mac might not be able to continue. He placed a hand on Mac's arm. "She would never have let any of us stay here, don't blame yourself." Tony knew the words wouldn't alleviate the guilt, they weren't helping his own. When he'd left Lucy and Mac had been with her. He never imagined she'd go to work alone.

"When I got here the back door was opened, and I walked in and found Henry."

While Mac spoke with Scott, Tony looked for something to do and saw the coffee pot filled. He remembered his first cup of coffee with Keeva. Right now he knew if he saw her, he'd tell her how much he loved her. How much he wanted to be with her, to drink coffee with her every morning, to have her in his and TJ's lives. An ache in his chest grew. He wanted to see her again and know she was okay. He had to let her know how he felt, that he'd support her.

"Wasn't there a patrol out front today?" Scott asked.

Scott's voiced pulled him out of reverie. "Yes, Jimmy was supposed to be here. We, I mean I, knew she and Jimmy were close, so I knew he'd watch out for her. But when the girl was attacked, he was called to the scene."

"What happened, Tony? Why did you send Mac here?" Scott asked.

"Because we found a vile of Versed at the scene and at the attack we had several weeks ago, we found a cap from a syringe. The syringe caps were the same type. It didn't take a rocket scientist to figure out there was a connection."

"But I thought the guy died in a car accident?" Scott's confusion was understandable.

Then the truth hit Tony. The notes in the pocket, the cap, the Versed, the attacks, it all began to make sense. "*Dios mio*." He slammed his fist on the counter. "That's it. That is what has been bothering me all night."

Mac and Scott looked at Tony like he had grown an extra head. "What are you talking about?" Scott was the first to speak.

Tony balled his fists and closed his eyes. He needed

to think, he needed to put this all together. "This guy has a medical background." He began pacing, walking in circles. "He has known where we would be, he used Versed, he knew to avoid us and used disguises. He's one of us." He looked between Mac and Scott and saw the beginnings of understanding on their faces.

"So you're saying this guy is a cop?" Scott asked.

"I'm not sure. But, no, I don't think he's a cop. Maybe dispatch. I just know he knows the system and something about medicine. He's avoided us, he has access to Versed and I think that is our angle. We need to know where that medication is coming from." Tony's feeling of helplessness drained, but he worried for Keeva.

"Um, I don't know much about your work," Mac interrupted, "but in my experience in the Marine Corp, especially Afghanistan," he paused, "our medics knew everything. They knew where everyone was at all times. Even if it was one medic in a unit, they were uncanny. You'd yell *medic*, and they were already on the way to help. Could this guy be someone in the same situation? Could he be a paramedic who knows where everyone is and knows how to obtain Versed?"

Tony was impressed with Mac's quick comprehension of the situation.

About six months ago, Tony had heard about medications stolen from the hospital pharmacy. He hadn't heard any details or the outcome of the investigation.

He knew most of the staff in the E.R. and dialed the hospital E.R.'s direct line. "St. Peter's E.R., Carol speaking, can I help you?"

Tony recognized the nurse. She had taken care of TJ when he had stitches. She was a grandmother and had made an admiring comment about Tony's role as a single parent.

"Carol, this is Tony Salazar. I need to find out some information about a theft in the E.R." Tony rubbed his head and hoped she could help. Do you know anything about that?"

"Evening, stranger," her voice sounded light and airy. "Yes, there was an incident about six months ago. A new pharmacy intern was involved, but I don't know the details. The hospital fired her, though she claimed she never took anything. Why do you need to know?"

"We think we have someone illegally using Versed, and I'm trying to pinpoint how he got his hands on it." Tony hesitated. He knew the hospital was a tight-knit community and looked out for one another. "We think the person might be involved in the medical system." His throat tightened as he croaked out the next words, "It's very important we find who might have those meds."

Carol didn't respond, and Tony worried she might not answer him. Maybe she wanted to protect the hospital. Then her words came out haltingly, "I'm not going to ever say this on the record, but those of us who worked that night think a paramedic was involved in this."

Tony heard her mumble what sounded like, "Damn it, what the hell," before she continued, "I can't prove any of this, Detective, but some of us who worked with this girl think she was bamboozled by this shyster."

"I get it. This is all off the record, none of that is important, but I need to know who the paramedic was. A teenaged girl was attacked and a young woman has been kidnapped and," Tony decided honesty was his best hope of finding Keeva, "this young woman is important to me. I need..." Tony's voice choked, and for the first time in his life he didn't care if the whole world knew how vulnerable he was, "I need to find her."

"I understand." A serious professional tone returned to her voice. "His name is Dillon Smith. I still see him around so she never blamed him. But we all think it was him."

"Thanks, Carol." Tony ended the call.

Tony now had a name, but nothing else. Could this guy have drugged Keeva? He looked at Scott, "We have a name, a paramedic. Dillon Smith."

"It's a start." Scott said the words as he pulled out his phone and began scrolling. "Found only one address with that name." He motioned Lisbeth over,

"We need to go check out this address. Tony and I will go, but I want you and Johnson as backup."

He looked at Tony, his eyes steely. "You able to keep this professional? I can't risk losing this case if we find her…hurt."

Tony swallowed the acrid taste of bile that rose in his throat. Right now he needed to use his training, he needed to maintain a calm composure. This was a mission and he needed to keep that focus in order to find Keeva. "I just want to find her. I'll let you handle him."

"Okay. We go by the book, I don't want this guy getting off because of emotions."

*

Keeva opened her eyes. She was on her side and couldn't move her arms. Something held them tight behind her back. She twisted her arms and it felt like a strong cloth, or tape. Maybe it was duct tape holding them. When she moved pain shot through her shoulders. She blinked and tried to figure out where she was. The last thing she remembered was that she was at work, but she didn't remember anything after that.

Her mouth felt dry, she wanted water. She lifted her head, the room began spinning and nausea rolled up her throat. She dropped her head and closed her eyes until it passed. "Is any one there?" her voice was a raspy whisper.

The pain in her back worsened so she tried to

readjust her position. A vision of Henry, bloodied on a floor flashed in front of her. Where was she and what had happened?

She closed her eyes to ease the dizziness and try and figure out where she was. If she was tied up someone had meant to keep her still. Maybe if they thought she was still asleep she'd have a better chance of escaping.

She had just put the first batch of pastries in the refrigerator when she had heard a knock on the door. Then nothing, she couldn't remember anything. The pain from her shoulder increased and shot across her back, aggravated by the position of her arms.

If she escaped. Is this how her life would end? No saying good-bye to Mac or Betty, leaving her business a complete failure and full of debt, never telling Tony she loved him? Like a wall of support, outrage pushed at her and she became determined to get out of this situation. This would not be how it ended. She would get out or die trying. She didn't want to have any more regrets.

Sinking back into the bed, she closed her eyes. If she could relax the spasm in her back, maybe she could move her hands enough to loosen what held her hands. First, she needed to figure out what happened. That might help her figure out where she was. Henry had knocked at the door. His voice had sounded shaky, but with Henry, one never knew what to expect. Other images flashed, like the clippings on an editor's floor, they were random and confusing. *Calm down, you can remember.* She pinched her eyes shut. She remembered answering the door and Henry's face had looked like he had seen a ghost. He was all white and pasty, and then a man stepped out of the dark.

Keeva tried to picture the man's face. Then she saw blood and remembered crying over Henry. He had been laying on the floor bleeding. The focus on the events had helped her relax her muscles, and her back spasm eased.

She wriggled her wrists. Nothing happened. She bent her elbows, separating her hands a little and she felt some space. She gradually could tell she was moving them a little more and she began to feel the tape loosening.

Something thumped outside the door. Keeva froze and closed her eyes. Light came in through the door and Keeva tried to keep her breathing slow and steady, even putting in a slight snore. Sweat dripped down her neck and she swore he could see her heart pounding in her chest. A vile smell filled the air.

She remembered who it was. He, that was it, it was a guy, the paramedic. He had come to her house when she found the note. She recognized the beady eyes; they were the eyes she had seen the night of the attack on Madison and Todd.

When she opened the door for Henry, he had

jumped out with the gun and shoved Henry inside, following behind him. He had a hat and what looked like a bad wig on, stringy hair hung down over his face. He wore a coat and not the hoodie, but she knew it was him. He pulled out a syringe and told Keeva to stand still or he'd shoot Henry.

He had smelled bad, like old clothes and sweat. She had backed away when he had stepped close to her. The same odor permeated her nostrils now. He had hollered, "Bitch, stand still!" And he'd grabbed her arm and pulled her to him.

Henry had lunged to grab the man's gun when he grabbed Keeva's arm and that's when the gun had gone off. Henry fell and Keeva had dropped to her knees over him. Something poked her and her arm began burning.

She didn't remember anymore until waking up a few minutes ago. So he drugged her. That much she had figured out. She told herself to keep breathing like a snore. He shone the flashlight on her face and she had to concentrate to keep still.

What seemed like an eternity later, the door shut but the odor lingered. She could hear him walking on the other side of the door.

Keeva's palms began sweating and her whole body began shaking. If he opened the door now, he'd know she was awake.

Her hands felt puffy. They had probably swollen a

little from the poor circulation. She stopped twisting them and tried relaxing again. What if she couldn't get past him?

The knife! She had put it in her pocket like she did everyday she worked. Could he have searched her and removed it? Moving backwards a few inches increased the pain in her shoulders and back, but it paid off. Something pressed against the inside of her back jean pocket, the knife. It was still there. Her T-shirt had hung over her hips, so he probably didn't notice it.

The renewed pain brought back the sweating in her neck and her hands. The tape loosened some more.

It seemed as if she had been trying to escape for hours, but soon she freed one hand. Her arm cramped when she pulled it loose. She gasped. The sound echoed in the quiet room.

Everything had remained quiet and she hadn't heard any noises since he had come in earlier. She wondered if he had left or gone to sleep. Maybe he knew she was freeing her hands and he was waiting in the dark for her to walk out.

Could he have a camera on her? Too late now, she had her hands out and pulled out the pocket knife. After cutting the tape from her feet, she dropped her legs over the side of the bed and lifted her upper torso. She felt weak, and the room whirled a little, but not as much as she had expected. Sitting up, she took slow deep breaths until the room seemed to stop moving.

*

They found the suspect's apartment empty. Tony wanted to punch someone or something. They weren't any closer to finding Keeva than they had been an hour ago.

"What the hell is going on? Why are they looking for Dillon?" Tony jumped at the sound of Jimmy's loud voice as he bound into the apartment.

"Calm down, son." Scott's voice controlled as he put a hand up to stop Jimmy. "I thought you were at the hospital."

"I was, but Kimberly's parents were taking her home already so… Why are you looking for Dillon?"

"Do you know Dillon Smith?"

"Yes, I know him. He's my half-brother." Jimmy stood in the middle of the studio apartment surrounded by fellow police and detectives. Like Lot's wife who turned to stone, they all froze and looked at Jimmy.

Tony spoke first. "Dillon? Dillon Smith is your half-brother?" The relationship between Tony and Jimmy had been contentious since Tony joined the department but Tony had always managed to walk away when Jimmy provoked him. Right now he wanted to kill the man. Had he known what his brother was up to and not said anything? He strode toward Jimmy.

Lisbeth stepped between them and spoke to

Jimmy. "We need to find Dillon, Jimmy. He might know something about Keeva or know who kidnapped her."

Jimmy looked at Lisbeth, his fist clenched. He opened his mouth, and then a startled look crossed his face. He paled. "Holy shit, it can't be."

Beads of sweat dampened his ashen white skin. His body began swaying. Lisbeth grabbed his elbow and led him to the couch, helping him to sit. "The cabin," he whispered.

Kneeling in front of Jimmy, Lisbeth placed a hand on his knee, "What cabin?"

"My cabin," he croaked. "He asked me to use it for a while. It doesn't get used much and he said he wanted to fix it up so he could spend the summer there." The color inched back up his face.

"You think he took Keeva there?" she asked.

"I didn't even know Keeva was missing. I knew something was going on, but I was busy at the hospital. When I got in my car I heard the chatter and the 10-23 so I called dispatch and asked where everyone was. She gave me this address and I thought something happened to Dillon."

Jimmy stood and interlocked his hands behind his head and blew out a breath. "When you mentioned Keeva it all clicked. Dillon had mentioned her several times. But when had told me he liked someone,

I figured it was a crush. He isn't the type of guy most girls liked." He shook his head. "I can't believe this."

The hell with the niceties, Tony wanted a location. "Where is the cabin, Smith? We think he has Keeva and need to get to her."

"Rimini. It's up Rimini Road. About a mile beyond the town, it's not too far off the road. My mom's family has had it for years and I inherited it. Dillon harbored some weird notion he should have gotten the cabin even though we are related through our father."

"Text me directions. I'm heading there." Tony headed for the door.

*

Keeva stood slowly, checking her balance and listening for the wood floor to groan. She turned to scan her surroundings. A sliver of light shone through one of two windows. They both looked like they had boards over them. She surveyed the rest of the room, while listening intently for any sound on the other side of the door. Besides the bare mattress, a blanket and a pillow, the room looked empty.

She turned the door knob, but it didn't move. With the knife still in her hand, Keeva sat back on the bed. She felt inadequate. If she had been stronger, she wouldn't be here.

Tears streamed down her cheeks, and a lump formed in her throat. An ache for her mother and father gripped her chest. She wondered if she would be in this mess if they were alive. It didn't matter; she was here and they weren't.

Sitting in the dark, Keeva remembered the first time she and her dad had gone hunting. She was twelve and had just taken her hunter's training, earning her junior hunter's license. It was a rite of passage to adulthood. When Mac turned twelve he earned his, and for the first time in her life, Keeva had been jealous of her brother. But several years later she had finally been old enough.

They had gone camping the weekend before hunting season had opened. Her father had said she needed to know more than basic safety and hunting skills. They didn't take anything but a little food and water. Paddy Ryan believed the land had been a gift from God and everyone living should respect all that came with this gift.

Though she had seen much of what he would teach her when she went hunting with him and Mac, he said she needed to learn to survive on her own. On the first night all they did was listen. Every sound they heard she had to identify. He had even sent her for water, alone. Or so she thought. She smiled at the memory. Later her father told her he'd followed her down to the stream.

When she came back to camp, she had to tell him everything she had heard and seen. At first she had balked, "Dad, how can I see, it's so dark."

"But there is light from the sky. Even on cloudy days, your eyes will help you see." He had Keeva close her eyes and sit quietly. In time, she had remembered enough it had surprised even her.

The second night she had heard large noises while she collected firewood. At the time not knowing her father had stood feet away with his shotgun ready. Bright eyes had twinkled between two bushes and her worst nightmare came true. She had come face-to-face with a mountain lion. She shivered remembering the fear she had felt. But her father's persistent training had kicked in and she had pulled the bear spray canister from its holder on her hip.

Raising her arms high and wide, holding the can like a weapon, she had growled, loudly, just as her father had taught her. Without taking her eyes from the animal, she had slowly backed up. Right into her father, who did the same as they moved back to camp.

Through the tears and shaking, she had told him how afraid she was. She had rambled about the whole incident, and how she could have died, except for everything he had taught her. He had reassured her they were fine. He then took her to all the traps and noise makers he had set around their camp.

"Inner strength let's you do the impossible in the worst of times me *inion*." A warmth touched her forehead, as though he were once again brushing her wild curls away while soothing her with his Gaelic. "Ye need to trust in ye'self, lassy. Ye were great, the bravest huntress."

The next two days she and her father had practiced other safety and survival techniques. After stressing preparedness being the most important, he had told her the element of surprise was the best in hunting and if she were ever in danger.

A calm came over Keeva as though her parents' spirits were there to comfort her. A sudden inner strength swelled in her chest along with the confidence that she could and would do this. She focused on the knife in her shaky hand. She would need to use that knife on the man who waited outside that room. Would she be able to kill a human? Hell, yes. This guy was a monster. Keeva crossed herself and asked for her parents and God's strength to get out of this.

Laying on the bed, Keeva rewrapped the tape on her feet. She hid the cut opening on the underside. Her plan required she sit up, so she ripped off a small piece from the tape that went around her wrists and secured her ankles enough to hold the tape in place. Though it looked secure, the tape was worthless as a restraint. As long as he couldn't tell, it didn't matter. She put her hands behind her back, shoving the rest of the duct tape under the pillow and gripped the knife.

"Help, help, is someone out there?" She didn't have to fake the shaky, fearful sound that escaped her mouth.

Nothing happened. "Help, please someone help me." She yelled louder. Afraid she'd pull the tape open at her feet she kept her legs still. She heard a screen door bounce shut. Her hands began sweating and she gripped the knife tighter. Dropping it was not an option.

Metal clinked on the other side of the door. Her mouth went dry when he stepped in the room. A light flashed in her face and she squinted. She forced her hands still before she threw them over her eyes.

"The l-light. It's hurting my eyes."

He moved it to the direction of the floor.

She started to lift her head, trying to keep turned slightly on her back to hide the knife. "Why am I here? Who are you?" She recognized the paramedic.

"You know me, Keeva. You saw me that night. Remember? You saved that girl and I knew it was destiny that we would be together." He leaned over her, he still smelled putrid. She peeked out of one eye. His hair looked thin and greasy.

"Oh, yes. I remember." She tried to keep her voice calm, but the dryness in her mouth made her sound a little hoarse. She remembered the day she had seen him at the café. "You stopped by the café, but left before I could speak to you."

A thin smile crossed his lips. Relief at his recognition boosted her confidence.

Her hands were shaking and sweating, and the

knife started to fall. She gasped and pulled it tighter. "Can you help me sit up? Please, my arms hurt."

He placed the flashlight on the bed next to her. Keeva cringed and held her breath trying to avoid the awful odor he emitted. She waited until he had his arms around her, but moved her head so her wild mane would block his vision of her hands. As he pulled her into a sitting position, she swung her arm around, and the small knife hit his back, she pushed and pulled toward her, making sure the knife didn't shut. It had a lock on it, but as old as it was it didn't always work.

He screamed and let go of her reaching for his back. Keeva was a few inches shorter than him but she outweighed him. She shoved him back. He came at her with both hands toward her throat. She put the knife low and up toward his mid-section. Less nervous, knowing she had wounded him, she thrust hard as it hit his skin.

His hands tightened on her neck, and Keeva felt her head throbbing. She pushed harder at the knife and twisted. His grip loosened a bit, and her hands, now wet with blood, slipped from the knife. Reaching up, she shoved at his shoulders. First, he just leaned in and pushed her harder against the bed, but she could feel his grip weakening.

Keeva grabbed at his hands, no longer squeezing tight around her neck. He started to fall down on her and she shoved him to the side. She grabbed the flashlight as she propelled herself off the bed. Running to the door, she could hear him behind her, "Bitch. I'll kill you." There was a thud. It sounded like he slid to the floor.

Exiting the room, she ran into the back of a chair, almost tumbling over it. She looked around the room in every direction but it was dark, except for slivers of light coming through a knothole in what looked like a boarded-up door. Where was the screen door she had heard?

She heard him behind her at the bedroom door's threshold, "You won't escape, you know." His voice was raspy.

An opening lead off the living area, and she hoped to the kitchen and the back door. She could feel the cold air as soon as she stepped into the small kitchen. The moon shone through a window and a crooked screen door. She didn't want to turn the light on and make it easier for him to find her.

Keeva went into a full sprint, out the screen door, hoping there wasn't anyone else out there. She tripped on something and fell on dewy wet grass. She could smell cigarette smoke. Shit, what if there were others?

Pushing herself up, her hand hit metal, it was a bucket and smoke wafted into her face. That must be where the smoke came from. Maybe it had been only him. Relief washed over her.

Something banged and rattled in the house.

Standing, she looked in all directions for a road or driveway. Remembering the boarded up door opposite the one she ran out, she ran around the house.

The moon lit up a long driveway that ended on a dirt road. A car sat out front. She doubted he left the keys in it and a peek in the window confirmed he hadn't. Her only option was to keep running and hide in the woods.

The tree line sat back about ten feet off the road on both sides of the street. She needed to gain distance from him. She bolted across the street. The road headed downhill in one direction and uphill in another. Downhill gave her better odds of finding a town or another house.

Outdoors was her element. She had often camped alone and spent many hours of her life hiking or running outdoors. She slowed her pace when she reached the dense forest. He was injured and she doubted he'd run after her, but he could still take the car. She had to be quiet and stay low. At first she wanted to run, but she had little visibility and risked tripping over the thick underbrush. She stepped carefully.

Spotting a juniper sandwiched between two larger pines she moved behind it. Keeva's chest felt like it was ripping in two and she needed to catch her breath. Her breaths came out in pants, and she doubled over to suck in air.

When her breathing calmed a little, she peered out

and she could see Dillon come around the side of the house. He stumbled to the car. Keeva didn't want to give away her hiding place so she stayed as quiet as her heaving chest would allow.

He fell against the hood of the car and disappeared down the side. Keeva wanted to rest more but didn't want to risk he'd come look for her. Crouched down, she took slow quiet steps deeper into the woods away from the road. The moon didn't offer as much light in the dense forest so she had to move carefully not to trip on the underbrush.

Her sweating had soaked her shirt and for the first time she felt the cold air. It had penetrated her damp clothing. The ground still had snow on it so she knew they were in the higher elevations, but with all the mountains that surrounded Capital City that could be anywhere.

There were piles of snow and she stepped in several that dampened her thin work sneakers. Her feet became as cold as the rest of her. She crossed her arms and rubbed her hands on her upper arms trying to create friction.

A car engine sounded from behind. She squatted down behind bushes and could see the headlights swerving back and forth. She didn't know if he was trying to find her or if she had given him enough injuries he was having trouble maneuvering.

CHAPTER 10

MAC FOLLOWED TONY to his car and said, "I'm going!" He dropped into the passenger seat and put on his seatbelt before Tony could say anything. Tony wanted to argue, but couldn't think of one other than it might cost him his job.

Scott walked out and signaled for Tony to wait up. Tony opened his window. "I don't want to stand here all day and figure this out."

"Damn it, Salazar. Don't you think I want what is best for her? If you go running in with guns blazing you both could end up dead. Dillon didn't hesitate to shoot Henry."

The reality hit Tony. Scott was right, if he did go in blindly he'd likely get himself or worse, Keeva, shot.

He pinched his lips and nodded. "You're right. But I can't wait around here too long."

"I understand your concern." Scott motioned Tony over to his car where other officers were waiting and outlined their next steps.

After they had outlined the plan, Tony got back into the car with Mac. Neither of them spoke as they drove to the rendezvous spot. They picked a destination that wouldn't allow Dillon to turn off any side streets. Two sheriffs' cars were going to drive up past the cabin and block him from exiting in that direction.

They pulled up behind Scott. He placed a map on the hood of his cars, several nearby police officers and sheriff's held flashlights over the map. He stepped aside for Jimmy. "The other two cars are stopping here." His finger landed on the nearest intersection. "It's not likely he would ever go in that direction because he risks getting stuck. Beyond the cabin, the road is only good in the summer. I have an old truck out there, but it hasn't been started in some time and I doubt it will. His sedan will never make it over any of that terrain."

Jimmy looked around and met Tony's gaze. They did a few second stand-off before Tony nodded his approval. He found it odd that Jimmy even cared if it mattered to him. Tony knew Jimmy and Keeva's friendship ran back to high school. Until now, Jimmy acted like it didn't matter what Tony thought. Or maybe Tony's opinion always mattered to Jimmy and Tony never noticed.

"We need to keep a few patrols here," he put his finger on the location where they stood, "and we have two waiting at the end of Rimini Road and Highway 12. If on some quirk he manages to get past the first two stops." He looked around at everyone. "Scott, Tony, Lisbeth and I are going to lead the way in."

"What about me?" Mac asked.

"Mac, we can't let you go in. Legally that puts us in shit up to our ears and we can't risk that." Jimmy answered too soon.

"It's my sister, Jimmy, and Dillon is your brother. How do I know you won't save him over her?"

Scott stepped between Jimmy and Mac. He spoke to Mac. "Listen, son. Jimmy isn't going in. He's going to lead us to the cabin. He knows the layout and we need him there. There are six others from the SWAT team going in, including Tony and myself. We will do everything we can to protect her."

Mac's eyelids lowered, and through the dim light of the flashlights, Tony could see his anger. He didn't blame him.

They all got in their cars. The intention was to drive with their lights off and get close to the cabin. Tony had tried his hardest to keep his focus on the mission, but this was more than personal. The unknowing was the hardest part. They didn't have any idea what they were going to find.

Their radio crackled. Scott answered his. Tony could hear the sheriff from the other end. "We're pulled off on a narrow drive at a deserted structure. We can see headlights heading in this direction. We are pretty well hidden by the overgrowth. Something is wrong. The car is swerving like a drunk on a binge."

"Roger. Stay out of sight and signal when he passes you. If it fits the description, block him in from the rear. " Scott radioed back.

Tony had driven in front of the other cars, and according to the plan, he would get Keeva and bring her out safely. He blocked all the thoughts distracting him from focusing and concentrated on getting Keeva out.

They drove slow not to kick up dust and had gone a quarter of a mile when the same sheriff came through their radios. "It's our perp. We'll block him from the rear."

As they spoke Tony could see lights bounce through the trees and then on the road. One of the officers parked his car perpendicular across the road. The road in front of them curved so the car would not see them yet. The other vehicles pulled out of the way. The officers exited their cars and moved into position behind their cars.

For the first time Tony noticed the night air chill

and saw the snow on the ground in the trees. He hoped Keeva was warm; the idea she was suffering in any way put an ache in his chest, and the pressure of tears built up. God, he loved her and didn't know if he could do a damn thing about it. The best thing he could do for her was to focus.

The car rounded the corner. It was going slow and driving erratic. It stopped as soon as it turned the corner and the police car was visible. The driver put it in reverse, but before he could move, six SWAT members, guns drawn, surrounded the car.

They dragged him from the vehicle and handcuffed him on the ground. He had blood all over his back. Tony didn't see anyone else in the car, but someone had already popped the trunk. It was empty.

Rage built inside him. Tony ran over to the handcuffed Dillon and flipped him over. There was blood covering his shirt and his face was pale. "Where the fuck is she?" Tony wanted to grab a hold of his throat, but someone grabbed him from behind.

"Chill, Tony." Lisbeth shoved him back.

The slimy bastard whispered, "You'll never find her."

Tony knew they had a half-mile from where they parked to the cabin and had gone about a quarter mile. He broke from Lisbeth's hold and grabbed Dillon again, "Where is she, slime bucket?" His voice was raspy in a loud whisper. Strong arms grabbed him and pulled him back. Tony didn't recognize the sheriff who shoved him with one hand and held out his Taser with the other. Tony wanted to pummel Dillon but knew he'd be down as soon as he made another move. Every minute Keeva went missing put her at greater risk of not being found alive. "*Conyo!*" Tony swore before taking swift strides to his car.

Dillon began laughing, a cackling laugh that penetrated the night air. Tony didn't know what he could do for Keeva, but he had to find her. He motioned to Scott he was leaving.

Scott called two SWAT team members and told them to follow in their vehicle. He drove slow, scanning the dark terrain for any signs Keeva might be around. A light flashed in the corner of his eye. It had been quick but he knew he saw a light. He pulled over and exited the vehicle. The two SWAT members were already walking up to him as Scott's car stopped behind theirs.

"There was a light about twenty yards into the woods. It could be Keeva or someone working with Dillon."

"What do you think we should do?" Scott said.

Tony appreciated Scott's support. They had worked many cases together and until tonight, Scott had never questioned or chastised Tony's judgment. "If the two of you head up about ten yards, then back track here, you'll have the rear flank covered. Scott and I will go in front of where we spotted the light."

Tony sliced his hand through the air in a signal to go. He waited several seconds for them to disappear in the thick forest and gave a sign for Scott to follow him. Between their dark SWAT outfits and the dense foliage, he knew only someone with specialized training could spot them. There had been no sign of a second person until he saw the light. Could Dillon be a diversion while someone took Keeva elsewhere?

Keeva's essence, the fiber of her being oozed kindness. No one who set out to hurt her deserved to take another breath. Consequences be damned, if she was hurt he'd do some serious damage to whoever harmed her. Silently stepping deeper into the tall pines, he could feel Scott step up behind him.

"You see anything?" Scott asked.

Tony stilled and breathed in the air. He could smell something besides the pine. His heart beat a little bit faster, he knew someone was there and he sensed it was Keeva. Behind them, they heard a snap. In unison and silence, they turned in the direction of the sound.

With the stealth of a cat, Scott moved several feet away. Understanding his reaction, Tony countered Scott's move in the opposite direction. From this angle, the moon shone on a small cluster of young pines and a shadow of a person crouched down among them. That must have been what propelled Scott to move.

In most missions, patience became one of Tony's strongest virtues. But not tonight. An urgency nagged at him and he wanted to move into get whomever squatted in those trees.

He looked around and spotted Scott and the other two team members. He pointed with his fingers for them all to move in. Stepping closer, the figure crouched lower and a long cascade of thick curls fell over the figure's shoulders.

Tony closed his eyes and breathed in a breath of relief, thanking every god out there. He held his arm up and hand flat to motion the others to stay back.

"Keeva?" He would know her anywhere.

She pushed aside the branches and stepped out. "Tony? Oh, Tony, you came. You came for me!" She jumped out of the bushes, wrapping her arms around his neck.

His arms wrapped around her and he could feel her. She was safe. Relief washed through Tony. He knew he could never let her go again, somehow he'd make it work.

Sobs wracked her chest as she cried and held on to him. He saw blood on her hands and arms. Some of it dried in her hair. "You have blood on you? Are you all right? Maybe the medics should take a look at you."

"I'm fine, I'm fine. Did they get him? Tony it was

awful, I had to…" Keeva's body shook in time with her renewed sobs.

"We got him, Keeva, we got him. "

The others moved around them. Scott turned on his flashlight and began leading them out. While they walked to the road, Tony pulled Keeva close. Her whole body began trembling. He pulled off his jacket and placed it around her shoulders. Scott was talking in his microphone. When they reached their cars, the lights from the approaching vehicles began lighting up the road.

An ambulance arrived and the paramedics jumped out, one came straight over to Keeva. She pulled back.

"It's okay, *chula*. You'll be safe with them, they're good people. They had nothing to do with the guy who took you." Tony whispered close to her ear. Tony felt lost on how to help her. A female medic came over and coaxed Keeva to the back of the ambulance. Tony stepped back to let them work.

Mac came up. "How is she?" He sounded panicked.

"She doesn't appear to be injured anywhere."

Tony knew he loved Keeva, in the darkness and in the light. Between the good and the bad, he loved her. She was strong, passionate, and most of all brave. He had to find a way to make it work.

He watched Mac go over and embrace Keeva. That was her family. Not Tony. She had told him she needed space. What she needed now was people she loved, and he wasn't one of them. He walked back down the hill toward his car.

*

Keeva watched as Tony walked away. It felt like a drain had pulled all her emotions and swept them away. She followed his movements in the sea of uniforms. Yesterday she had told him a relationship was impossible, now she regretted it.

Mac's comfort felt good but it didn't assuage the hurt she felt. "Mac, I'm so glad you're here."

"An army couldn't keep me away." He pulled back, holding her arms out. "Are you okay?" He turned her hands over, focused on them. "What is this blood? Were you hurt?"

"No, I'm fine. That's the creep's blood."

"What happened to him? He's hurt, but they weren't sure if he was shot or stabbed." He tilted his head and looked at her.

"Stabbed." The realization of it all hit Keeva. Chills ran through her muscles and she began shaking. "I...I used my pocket knife. The one Dad gave me, like yours. It was all I had." Her own voice sounded foreign and faded.

Mac pulled her close. "You did good, sis. You got him. He'll never hurt you again."

"I lost the knife. Maybe the police will find it." She spoke to Mac but looked for Tony. Walking through the woods, she had promised herself as soon as she saw Tony she'd tell him how she felt. But she cried and rambled instead.

"Don't worry about the knife. I can give you mine. Hell, I'll give you my K-Bar."

Keeva looked up at her brother, his curls hung in his face. She smiled. "It was weird, Mac. I was thinking about Dad and the first time we went hunting alone. That's when he gave me the knife. And, it was as though," she paused, remembering what happened in the cabin, "he was there with me. I felt him, I could swear I heard him talking and he told me what to do. He told me how to be strong."

Mac leaned over her, kissing the top of her head. "I'm sure he was there, little sis."

*

Keeva had insisted on seeing Henry when they got to the hospital. They had told her he was fine but because of his age, they were keeping him overnight for observation. She opened the door to his room and peeked in. A dim light shone upwards over his bed, casting an eerie glow over his pale face. She walked over and placed her hand on his chest, then gulped. He was alive but guilt still pushed her to touch him and reassure herself. She pulled up a chair and sat by the bed.

Henry opened his eyes and his face brightened. "Hi, Mizz Keeva. They got you back." His look turned sour. "I'm so sorry. I didn't do too good. I let him take you." He started crying

Careful of his IV, Keeva patted his hand. "No, no, you did fine, Henry. He shot you when you tried to protect me. And we're both fine, so don't worry." His innocence overwhelmed her. Keeva stroked his arm.

"I hope Mizz Betty don' get mad at me for not protectin' you." His scowl almost made Keeva laugh.

"You tried and that's what matters. Don't worry, she isn't mad at you. I spoke to her a little while ago and she was worried about you. In fact, she wants you to come stay with her the next few days. Her other room has a bed that comes down from the wall and she wants to take care of you."

Henry's mouth formed a perfect O-shape that matched the roundness of his widened eyes. "I don' want to cause her no trouble."

"It's okay. It will give her something to do and besides she has a proposition."

"What's a proposhun?"

"I think she wants to make you an offer. The small apartment next to hers is going to be empty, and she'd like to have you near her." She waited but he looked blankly at her. "She is going to rent it for you." Keeva knew Henry would have to take time to absorb this. She figured he might as well plant the seed.

"Oh, I can't let her do that. I have some social

money I get every month. But it ain't enough for the fancy place Mizz Betty lives in."

Keeva rested her chin on the bed's side rail. She was tired, but Betty had asked her to reassure Henry she would take care of him. If he had to leave the hospital and needed care, they would put him in a nursing home and Betty didn't want that. "Miss Betty can afford it. The only family she has is you, Mac and me. I think it would help her to have you near her." Keeva waited before breaking the next news. "But if you go there, you can't walk around at night."

He tilted his head and his eyebrows drew together. "Okay. I bet that fancy place's got rules to keep it fancy."

Henry laid back and looked at the ceiling before turning back to Keeva. "I guess I should stay by Mizz Betty. All the years she helped me, and if she needs some company I can do it. But there's something else." A pained look crossed his eyes. "But what about you, Mizz Keeva? Who'll watch the café?

A cry almost escaped her mouth at his concern. Keeva placed her hand over her mouth to hide her reaction. She removed her hand and had to swallow before she could speak. "I'm not going to need anyone to watch the café. They have the bad man. I won't have any more problems there."

Henry didn't respond.

"What is it, Henry?"

"I know you'll be busy all the time. But could you still sometimes bring me rolls? I bet they don' have rolls as good as yours."

If Betty hadn't offered to take Henry, she would have after that. "I will bring you whatever you want. And with you and Betty in the same place, I'll be visiting a lot."

After finishing his reports, Tony came by the hospital to check on Keeva and found Mac who sent him to Henry's room. After what appeared to be several long minutes, the door started to inch open. She stepped out backwards and waved pulling the door shut. Without looking back, she began walking in the opposite direction of where he stood. She didn't see him.

Tony wondered if he should let her go, let her live her life in peace. No, he had to try. At least he would tell her he loved her. "Keeva."

Keeva jumped and turned. He saw surprise in her eyes. "Wow, you startled me. I hadn't seen you there."

"I'm sorry. Mac told me where you were. I…I needed to talk to you."

Tony felt like his hands were in the way, so he stuck them in his pockets. The words once again, all jumbled in his head. She stood there looking so magnificent even with everything that had happened to her today.

"Is everything all right? She walked up to him.

He could see purple smudges under her eyes. When he first met her, she'd looked tired *and* like a goddess. Things had not changed.

"I know this isn't the time. You've had one hell of a night and you probably just want to go home and sleep, but I…"

She surprised him when she took his hand. "What is it, Tony?"

He squeezed her soft hands in his two big fists. "*Chula*, I know you deserve better than me. I know I'm like a Stone Age brute when it comes to machismo… but I've been trying to find what is important… But I've realized that what I need is right here, right in front of me. You are the most beautiful, brave and sweetest woman I have ever met. You amaze me. What I am trying to say is, I love you, Keeva Ryan."

Tears streamed down Keeva's cheeks, and Tony wished he had kept the words to himself. She looked at him in confusion, biting her lip. Oh, crap, had he blown it again? Then he saw her lips turn into a hint of a smile.

"I love *you*, Tony Salazar." Keeva's voice was husky and the tears were flowing freely.

He blinked. Tony couldn't believe the words he heard. She loved him? He wrapped his arms around her and covered her round soft mouth with his lips. God, he had missed her.

Keeva sighed when Tony moved away. "You are

beautiful and I plan on finishing that kiss and ravishing your body. But right now I want to get you home, where we will both sleep for the next twenty-four hours."

Keeva was smiling and put an arm around his waist as they walked toward the waiting room. He put an arm over her shoulders.

In the waiting room they found Mac asleep across a row of chairs. One of Mac's feet hung down on the floor. Tony kicked it. "Rise and shine, Sleeping Beauty. It's time to go home."

Mac lifted his hand off his eyes and his mouth beamed. "It's about time you two figured it out." He stood and shook Tony's hand. "Glad you'll be sticking around."

Tony looked at Keeva and grinned. "I plan to stick around for a very long time."

The trio walked into the fresh air just as the sun's rays peaked over the mountains. Sparkles of yellow, surrounded by wisps of pink and orange hues, lit the dark night sky with a promise of another big blue sky.